Take Me Back to Cairo

A Novel

Pamela Paterson and Tarek Hussein

ISBN: 978-1-7782304-2-4 (Paperback)
ISBN: 978-1-7782304-3-1(Ebook)

Book design by Katia Zuppel
Cover design by Yvonne Parks at PearCreative.ca

Printed by IngramSpark

First printed edition 2023

Writer Types Inc., Kingston, Ontario, Canada

Dedicated to two notable Canadian writers who inspired and mentored me: Governor-General award-winner E.D. Blodgett and my great-grandfather Georges Bugnet. Also dedicated to Alex Sawchyn, my junior high English teacher who kept believing in me.
—Pamela Paterson

Dedicated to the two women closest to my heart: my mother, Amal, the first and best storyteller I've ever known, and my wife, Pam, my biggest fan who brought out the storyteller in me by agreeing to co-write this story.
— Tarek Hussein

Praise for Take Me Back to Cairo

"Pamela Paterson and Tarek Hussein have written a rollercoaster of a love story that triumphs over a collision of cultures, family dynamics, an old lover, and new traditions. From Kingston to Cairo and back again, this is a compelling and heartwarming tale by two writers who clearly know the inside story."
– Terry Fallis, two-time winner of the Stephen Leacock Medal for Humour

"With a high sense of humor and deep knowledge of the characteristics of Egyptian and Canadian cultures, Pamela Paterson and Tarek Hussein wrote a precious book about the two mentalities in the diversity frame. The writers took me smoothly to the depth of both cultures as they appeared in the behaviour, thinking, and feeling of the characters. The style, structure, and development of the action in this piece of fiction made me murmur: this intelligent way of writing is worth reading for its enjoyment and benefit."
– Jamal Saeed, author of Yara's Spring and My Road from Damascus

CHAPTER 1

When I saw the call coming in, I knew it was another call to pressure me to return to Egypt. Mom was determined to line up cousin after cousin, finding cousins I'd never even heard of until I agreed to marry one of them. Luckily, it was my stop, and I could have this conversation off the bus. I stepped out the back door onto Ontario Street and pulled up the collar of my camel hair coat. The cold wind still slipped in.

"Good morning, Mama," I said. "May God's blessings be upon you."

"Inshallah," she said. "You sound like you're outside, son. I hear traffic. Are you eating street food? It's not healthy or clean. Your dad got sick on street food and never ate outside again."

If Mom knew how often I ate street food, she might fall ill as if she'd eaten it herself.

"No street food for me. Too dangerous."

"Thank God, son," Mom said. "You need home food, delicious and nutritious like what I used to cook for you."

"Mom, I love your food. I feel your love come through. And I'll have it again soon, Inshallah."

"You're so alone in Canada, son," she said.

I winced. As if peering into my mind, Mom said, "Yousef, Mohamed is temporary. May God bless him but you can't live with your cousin forever. Who will take care of you? Wash your clothes? Cook for you?"

"I'm doing fine. I have clothes. I'm eating," I said. "I eat with Mo and his family many times."

"Will they take care of you for the rest of your life?"

"Mom! I have to go. I'll speak to you soon, Inshallah."

As I stepped off the curb, a motorbike screamed by, so close that the handlebar grazed my hand as it sped away. "Donkey!" I yelled. "Screw you!"

The driver glanced briefly behind, then continued down Queen Street and turned left, disappearing completely. I still heard the engine screaming, though the image of that stupid pink helmet roared even louder through my head.

"Son! Son!" Mom yelled out. "Who are you shouting at?"

I loosened my tight grip on the phone. "Mom, I'm okay. I'm sorry I scared you."

"Yousef, what happened? Are you all right?"

"I'm fine, through God's graces. A motorcycle came by."

I couldn't tell Mom that I almost got hit. She'd insist that I come back to Egypt.

"A motorcycle? Oh my God, my son almost died," Mom wailed. "Canada seems too dangerous for you, son."

"It came by quickly and scared me."

"I know when my son is frightened," she said. "It sounds like you almost died. Why don't you let Mohamed drive you?" she asked.

"Mom, please, I don't want to depend on Mo for everything. He's already driving Rasha and the kids around. The minivan is full."

Besides, at thirty-three, why would I want to be in the back of a minivan with three kids, soon to be four, driven around like a little kid.

"Yousef, what will you do when the snow comes? We see it on the news all the time."

"Mom, it's ten degrees now."

"Ten degrees in May? I shiver every time you tell me the temperature. Are you wearing enough clothes, my son? Our Pharaonic genes are not meant to live in a freezer."

"No, Mom, it's fine. I'm fine." But somehow being reminded of the cold made me colder. I stretched my hat even further over my ears. Across the street, the Wolfe Island ferry dock was empty of the large ferry, allowing the wind to tunnel to me in a clear path.

"Yousef, it's thirty degrees and so beautiful here."

Even at thirty degrees, with millions of cars emitting thick smog Cairo is hardly a beautiful beach on the Red Sea. At that moment I tasted the black smog, coughing at its invasion of my throat and nostrils. I wouldn't trade this fresh Kingston air.

"Cairo is indeed beautiful."

"Please let Mo drive you," she pleaded. "at least until you come back. It won't be long, Inshallah. I'll talk to him."

"Mom, I'll handle this, please, Inshallah."

Mo apparently was the family expert in everything Canada after only five years, even shortening his name to Mo to appear religiously neutral while he prayed five times a day and watched Arabic media nonstop.

No point in arguing with Mom right now. I reached Pan Chancho Bakery and really needed to warm up.

"Okay, Mom? Say hi to Dad and my favorite sister."

Mom laughed. "Your only sister. Salam, son."

"Salam," I said as I entered the bakery's doorway.

Mom loved me deeply, but to her, I was still a boy who needed to be directed at every step. And she was more formidable than most mothers. She could easily lead a thousand men into a battle in the desert—with lipstick on and her hair done underneath her hijab.

My only hope was to stay an ocean away from her.

CHAPTER 2

The piles of fresh-baked bread and pastries stacked on the racks grabbed my nose and pulled me in as soon as I entered the bakery, reminding me of the large tray of pastries and sweets Mom would order from the French patisserie.

The hostess at her stand waved me over with a menu in hand. "How about some hot breakfast? Nippy out there." she smiled.

I had never heard the word "nippy" before. Was it always "nippy" or was it sometimes "nip"? Or "nipped"?

"Sorry, inside is full. Is the terrace okay?"

My jaw tightened. My other alternative, microwaved falafels, didn't appeal to me this morning. My stomach would surely riot if I tried to feed it another dose. Someday I'd learn how to cook, but now my stomach followed her outside, she in her T-shirt and me in my winter coat. Not sure how long a breakfast could even stay hot outside, eggs turning into cubes before they reach the table, like me.

She stopped at a table beside a window, where I'd have a full view of all the warm people inside, and placed the menu on the table, saying the server would be right with me. Right, not left, my tongue tossed around silently. I declined the water she offered, noticing she turned the "t" into a "d," as Americans do.

Mo said Canadians speak American English, not the British English we learned, but I should never compare Canada to the U.S. like it's one region. They have their own quiet pride, separate culture and country. A bit like being called a Saudi just because we're from the Middle East. He had a point. I'd only want to be called a Saudi if I got all those oil privileges.

At home, I'd be having this meal with somebody else. Eating alone just wasn't right. Even tea service is a shared event, formally served on a silver tray with milk and sugar containers and steeped to medium red in a clear glass with a handle. Getting used to drinking weak coffee from a cardboard cup with a plastic lid that dripped would take some time.

Tables were covered with bits of dried leaves and the umbrellas were stacked up in the corner, yet to be called into service. The only sign of anybody else was at the table next to me. A cup, book, and black jacket hanging on the chair. On one of the chairs was—could it be? A pink helmet.

My heart picked up pace and heat fired up in my body. It *could* be the same man who almost hit me. It was nearby, after all, and he was going in this direction. How good God is. Just then, a woman sat down and opened her book and the server appeared.

"Have you decided?" she asked.

"What's the best menu item without pork?"

"Huevos tostadas. It's an egg wrap, Mexican style. Hands down."

Unlike Mo, I wasn't afraid to try new foods. He'd probably never eat this thing that I can't pronounce.

"Whatever that is, if it's hands down, then that's what I need, thank you," I said.

"Coming right up." The server wrote down my order and went inside.

"Coming right up," I repeated to myself, turning it over and over as if it would soon make more sense. It's coming, but it's right, then it's up. Google said "hands down" meant without a doubt: when horse jockeys were so far ahead in the race, they could put their hands down and relax the reins. This local dialect still didn't make sense, so I returned my gaze to the woman and her book, peering over the rim of my coffee cup.

She had medium-length brown hair, high cheeks, and an all-too-regular nose. She was younger than me, maybe in her twenties. Black pants tucked into tall heavy black boots. Her clothing was rugged, but her demeanor was silent. She could easily fade into her surroundings, quiet as a stone.

After two cups of coffee, her husband still hadn't returned. Finally, I couldn't contain my thoughts. "Pardon me, I'm sorry to bother you, but is your husband coming back soon?"

She looked up from her book. "What?"

"Your husband," I repeated, wondering if my accent was too strong. "Your h-u-s-b-a-n-d."

"I heard you, but I don't know what you're talking about."

Her ring finger was bare. My cheeks became hot. How silly of me not to figure it out. One cup of coffee. One jacket. One helmet.

"I'm so sorry. I didn't mean to intrude. It's just that—"

"That what?"

"I almost had a terrible motorcycle accident this morning and I thought the pink helmet was the same person. Somebody almost killed me."

"That was you?" She bent the page in her book and closed it. "Why would you go against the walk light?"

"The walk light?"

"The walk light. The little white man. He lets us cross the street." She leaned forward. "I would've felt terrible if I hit you."

"So terrible you kept going?"

"You seemed okay. There was other traffic behind me. I'm sorry, okay?"

She picked up her book again and opened it to the folded page. In Egypt this would've been a much longer conversation, full of a thousand apologies and God's blessings said one way and another.

"I never thought almost killing me would be treated so casually."

"Look, I already said I'm sorry. I'm sorry that you don't know what a walk light is, but even a squirrel knows how to cross the street. Have you ever seen them? Dancing back and forth on the sidewalk until it's safe?"

So now I was being compared to a rodent.

"You're not from here, I can see that," she continued, leaning toward me. "You can only cross the street when you press the button, and the white walking man comes on. It was flashing the orange hand."

Pushing buttons. White walking man. Orange hand. There's no such system in Egypt. Crossing the street in Cairo is a careful and dangerous art that we must perfect at a young age. And it's true that I wasn't paying attention, talking with Mom. Besides, Mo said not to get into any hassles, or I could get deported.

"If I did something wrong, my apologies. I didn't intend—"

"It's fine," she said, cutting me off. "It happens."

The woman had already returned her focus to her book. How casual and pragmatic these people are.

Just then, a tiny bird with a reddish breast landed on a table beside the woman. My outrage diffused instantly. In truth, I wasn't proficient at being angry.

The tiny birds in my parents' back terrace, of which there were many, danced high among the trees. Mango, guava, banana, and lemon. When I pulled a branch toward me to pluck the fruit, they flew away, only returning when the leaves ceased rustling. Mom was wise to plant trees in the desert soil, barricading against the flying sand and air pollution.

How this little bird hopped around so gracefully, so light and beautiful, hopping onto another table then onto the ground then back again onto the table with such ease, his little head jerking this way and that way.

Slowly, I slid my phone out of my winter coat and aimed the camera at the bird. But it didn't stand still for its photo. I clicked away as it jumped around, from the table to the ground, then back. It hopped onto the woman's table, and I clicked again.

The woman stared at me. "Are you taking a picture of me?"

"Oh, no, I wasn't." The tips of my ears felt like the sun burned them. "My apologies, I was—"

Her face broke into a large smile. "I'm just teasing. I like birds, too. I like nature. I'm going on a motorcycle trip around New York State, hope to see some nice sights."

"Alone?" I asked, to be sure I understood. I'd only seen women like this in American movies—bold, courageous, and independent, willing to follow their own path in life.

"Unless you'd like to come with me. I have room on the back," she said, pointing her thumb behind her.

The server then appeared with my huevos tostadas and a coffee refill. I was grateful for the interruption. Was she flirting with me? How could I tell what these Canadian women were up to? I hoped she was flirting. I also hoped my face wasn't as red as the hot sauce.

Eating the food would be a good decoy while I regrouped. A small bite lets my mouth adjust to the heat. Good, even if much spicier than the beans I was used to. I can't keep talking to a woman without introducing myself.

"My name is Yousef Fahmy Ahmed El Sherif. Pleased to meet you. What is your good name?"

The woman hesitated, then extended her hand. "Janelle."

Her handshake was firm, almost hurting. How could somebody her size be so strong? Maybe it was from driving that motorcycle. At last, she let go. My arm felt exercised. I ate quickly trying to figure out what to do next.

"Where are you from?" Janelle asked.

"Cairo."

"I see. That makes sense now. Everything makes sense," she said, scanning me and nodding. "Your accent. Your look. Your camel hair coat. Did you shear off the camel yourself?"

"I don't understand."

"You know, shear it off and make a camel hair coat. That's what you're wearing, isn't it?" she said, pointing to my winter coat.

"Yes, you're right. It's a camel hair coat, but I didn't make it. I don't own a camel."

Most Egyptians don't own camels, and we rarely saw them in Cairo, except at the camel market or near the Pyramids for tourist rides.

Janelle laughed. I enjoyed how she didn't keep her laugh inside but gave it all to the world around her.

"Where are you from?" I asked.

"Toronto," Janelle said.

I hoped she wouldn't ask where I lived, like a teenager in my cousin's basement.

"Toronto is one of my favorite cities, although I don't know it very well. I landed in Toronto a few weeks ago."

"You're really fresh, aren't you?" she said, sliding her book away. "What do you like about Toronto?"

"I like cities—the energy, nightlife. I like the busy people. And Toronto is the right size for a city, not twenty million like Cairo."

"Yeah, three million must be like a small town to you. How do you find this cold weather? No desert heat here."

I shrugged. "I'm wearing my underpants today."

Janelle snorted. "Your what?"

"My underpants," I said, patting my leg.

"Thermals," Janelle said. "Good for you. I wish I had underpants on. It's cold on the bike."

Janelle stood up. "Nice to meet you, Yousef, but I need to get going. I'm catching the ferry."

My first conversation with a Canadian was over already. Life is freer here. Conversations between men and women are not bounded by strict social structures. I retrieved a business card from my wallet and handed it to her.

"My cell phone. It would be a pleasure to speak with you again."

Janelle buried the card in her front pocket. She hesitated, then snatched my phone off the table, added her phone number and email to my contact list, and handed it back to me. What a bold move!

I opened her contact card and read out her phone number: "Six hundreds and forty-seven, five hundreds and fifty-five, six hundred and eighty-one, five."

Janelle laughed. "It's 646-555-6815."

I repeated the number.

"Now you've got it. Okay, gotta run! Nice chatting with you." She bundled up her pink helmet, book, and jacket, and waved goodbye.

Before I could wish her a good day and ask for a chance to see her again, Janelle was gone.

CHAPTER 3

The clothes I laid out last night waited for me. How quickly my life was moving in the right direction; yesterday I signed a job contract with Mo's pharmacy, and today I'd be helping customers with their health.

The dress I chose fits in perfectly with my first day at work: custom-made navy blue wool pants and a burgundy button-down Burberry. Not too formal, but not too casual, either. Paired with my Italian leather shoes, I felt comfortable and confident checking the mirror one last time.

I mapped the bus route three times and set my alarm two hours earlier. Even though Mo offered to drive me, taking the bus was a small step toward independence. On the bus going downtown, I felt like a real working person with all the others. I had a purpose to my days now. I'd soon learn my new job and begin the recertification process. It'll take some time, maybe a year. Still, I'll be a pharmacist again without all of the encumbrances of a corrupt system, government auditors coming around saying they'd "help me" pass the review but knowing it just meant dipping into my pockets.

Inside the Kingston Centre grocery store, spotting the large pharmacy sign was like going through a portal that I couldn't turn back from—not that I wanted to. Finding a pharmacy in a grocery store was strange, but it was still a nice contrast to hospital-smelling pharmacies, whose phenolic smell lodged in my nose for weeks afterward. Mo was standing underneath the prescription drop-off sign, his growing chubbiness showing itself under the white coat. Rasha was such a good cook.

"Salam, Mo," I said. "With your white coat on, I barely recognized you."

Mo laughed. "Salam. Welcome." Mo swung open the gate, pointing at the turned back of a gray-haired woman on a stool wearing a blue lab coat. "Sandra is our registered pharmacy technician here. She'll show you your job today," he said. "Sandra, Yousef is here."

Sandra spun around and leaped toward me. Her well-lined face exploded with more lines when she smiled. "Yousef! Nice to meet you." She grabbed my hand in a tight handclasp that I jerked away from. Canadian women had such firm handshakes; it was almost a wrestling contest.

"I'll be training you," she said. "There's a blue coat and name tag in the back for you."

I didn't know I'd be trained by a woman, especially a technician. I suppose I didn't mind. Just surprised that Mo is letting a technician train a pharmacist. My eyes attempted to connect with his, but Mo didn't look up from his paperwork. Instead, Sandra pointed to the back, waiting for me to pass her.

Slipping on the blue lab coat, I affixed my name tag. 'Yousef' might be too difficult for customers. I should shorten my name to sound more Canadian like Mo did. I covered up the last three letters of my name tag. "You" might be easier, but would it be more confusing?

"I gave my prescription to You," customers would say.

"Who?"

"You."

"You didn't give it to me."

Bad idea. Maybe I should change my name to the English version "Joseph." Or even "Joe." For my customers, Joe would be so much easier than Yousef.

Sandra bellowed from the front, "Yousef! Are you done back there? It doesn't take that long to put on a coat. I need you up here."

I shouldn't be concerned about my name right now. "Coming," I called back.

Sandra, not rising from her stool, pointed to the stacks of boxes. "These totes came in today. Can you unpack them? Here's the scissors. You also need to verify all the contents and price the items with the stickers. Mo said you were a pharmacist, right? So, this should be easy."

She swiveled around, saying, "The new bottles go behind so we sell the existing product first. Separate the ones that go behind the counter."

I stared at her blue back. Mo was talking to a customer at the pick-up window. I guess it was okay to open boxes on my first day.

I cut open the first tote, reviewing the bottles and comparing them to the hundreds of shelf labels. How would I know where to put them? I didn't know what their system was. This pharmacy was arranged so differently.

"Excuse me, Sandra, where does this go?" I asked, holding up a big bottle of Senokot.

Sandra squinted, holding the bottle close to her eyes. "It's a brand name. It goes on that shelf on the right," she said, pointing.

Retrieving another bottle, I asked her again. Sandra exhaled loudly, the released air propelling her swivel. "It's Zyloprim. It goes on the generics shelf on the left. And don't put it in the Z section. It's Allopurinol and should be placed in the A section."

I felt like a child. A junior person, maybe even a high school student, should do this task. Not a pharmacist.

"Yousef," Sandra said, swiveling around, "I'm sorry, I don't mean to be bossy, but this is a busy pharmacy. One of the other technicians will finish unpacking the totes. I need you to do some cleaning next."

Cleaning? I'd never cleaned before in my life. Pharmacists aren't cleaners. It's not even hygienic.

Sandra handed me a bucket and washcloth. "Can you clean the bathroom?"

I stared at her. "What?"

"The b-a-t-h-r-o-o-m," she said slowly. "It's beside the backroom."

Mo was nowhere to be seen. Sandra flicked her hands as if to get rid of a fly. "Yousef, you've got to move faster. We're a busy pharmacy."

Dragging one foot behind the other, each step more degrading than the last, I slipped on a pair of pharmaceutical latex gloves. Then another.

Scrubbing the sink to the point where it gleamed and my fingers ached, I sprayed the mirror with glass cleaner, making circular motions with paper towel as I'd seen my parents' kitchen staff do, careful not to leave streaks. Mom hated streaks. Oh, how she'd tease me now. All my big ideas to get a new life in Canada, and I was demoted to one of the lowliest jobs in the world.

The yellow rings and specks of filth in the toilet taunted me, the smell permeating my nostrils and skin. I held back the urge to vomit.

"Sandra!" I called out. "Do you have any masks?"

Laughing came back. So, cleaning a toilet was funny? Give the crappy jobs to the new pharmacist. Was that how it worked?

"If you want your damn toilet cleaned, I'll clean it." I gripped the toilet brush with its splayed bristles and circled the bowl, flushing continuously. The water and the filth swirled around, disappearing down the hole.

Some yellow remained. I scrubbed harder and faster, determined not to let a toilet defeat me. In defiance, it splattered water, soaking my pants and lab coat.

"Dammit! Dammit!" I'd just dry-cleaned those pants. As I reached for the paper towel, the roll fell into the toilet, splashing me again. Dammit!

It quickly became waterlogged, too heavy to lift out with the toilet brush. Taking a deep breath, I reached inside and rescued the paper towel. Now I was infected with millions of bacteria hitching a ride on me. Stupid toilet.

"Yousef," Mo said from behind me.

I immediately straightened up, dropping the toilet brush and getting splashed again. I sighed.

"Sandra is on lunch. I need your help out front, please."

Discarding the gloves, I scrubbed my hands and smothered them with sanitizer.

"As customers come to the drop-off area, take their prescriptions and tell them it'll be forty-five minutes, okay?" Mo asked. "I'll be working on the computer over here. If they want anything else, call me. Are you comfortable with that?"

"No problem, Mo. I'll take care of everything."

Me and my wet pants stood at the drop-off counter, smiling at customers who strolled by with their grocery carts. Most of them barely noticed me, and the ones that did returned an uncomfortable forced smile. I casually leaned against the counter instead and texted Janelle.

Hi Janelle, I hope you are having a wonderful trip. I hope to see you again soon. Yours respectfully, Yousef.

Janelle texted back right away.

Thank u for your message. I loved the trip. N.Y. is gorgeous. I hope u r having a great day.

Hanging onto that moment, clasping my phone, my thoughts were broken by an elderly man ringing the bell.

"I have a bit of a scratchy throat. Looking for some cough drops."

"Cough drops," I repeated. Never heard of that. Cough syrup, sure. Ear drops, of course.

"They're usually near the cash," the man said.

"I'm sorry. It's my first day." Never admit you don't know something or customers will lose respect for you.

"Here they are, right under my nose," the man said, placing a package of lozenges on the counter. "Can I pay for it here or with my groceries?"

"With your groceries," I advised, turning my head away from the computerized cash machine and reaching for the ringing phone. "Good morning," I said, "May I help you?"

"Hi, is Sandra there?" a woman asked. "This is Marlene McNeil. I dropped off a prescription for Doug. Is it ready?"

"What's dog's last name?" I asked, scanning the counter around me. Typically, filled prescriptions would be bundled together in the same basket.

There was a pause on the line. "McNeil."

Just then, another customer approached the counter. I held up my hand to him.

"Can you spell?"

"M – C – N – E – I – L."

"I'll leave a message for Sandra. Thank you," I said, hanging up the phone. Dog prescriptions at the pharmacy! I'll laugh with Mo about this later, though it's not surprising given Westerners buy dog jewelry and clothes.

"Hello sir. May I help you?"

"My ear is hurting. It's inflamed," the man said, lightly touching his left ear. "What do you recommend?"

"Amoxicillin. I just unpacked some this morning," I said, taking it off the shelf. "It's the first treatment for bacterial ear infections."

"How much should I take?"

"It comes in five hundred milligram capsules. You need to take one capsule every eight hours for seven days."

Mo suddenly appeared beside me, grabbing the amoxicillin from my hands. "Sir, I'm sorry, but I'd advise you to get a prescription from your doctor first. There may be other issues that are going on, and this might not be the only treatment you need."

"Then why would he give it to me?" the man asked, gesturing an open hand toward me.

I stepped back from the counter.

"It's usually the first line of treatment for ear infections, but I'd advise you to check with your doctor first."

The man furrowed his brows, rubbed the back of his neck, then walked away. With the customer out of sight, Mo said, "Yousef, we don't diagnose and give medications without prescriptions—ever. I could lose my license."

"Mo, I'm so sorry, but in Egypt, you know, patients come to us for medical advice."

"Because they can't afford a doctor," Mo said, "But not here. Look at the amoxicillin bottle. What do you see before the name?"

"Rx," I said.

"That means it needs a prescription. Okay? If you don't know, ask me," he said in a firm voice. "Sorry for leaving you alone. Sandra is on her lunch and I got stuck on the phone with Rasha, then head office."

Placing his hand on my shoulder, Mo said, "Don't worry. You'll get it."

Mo's hand disappeared inside his pocket, where he kept his prayer beads. "Inshallah," he said.

"Inshallah," I responded.

"By the way, Rasha told me her sister is coming soon. She can bring any documents you need for your certification."

One positive point of the day.

CHAPTER 4

I dreaded coming home from my motorcycle trips, even one as fantastic as this one to New York State, riding along the picturesque shores of Lake Ontario. What would be waiting for me at home? It was always a new girlfriend of Daniel's for a long time, but for several months it's been the same stupid Meghan hanging around.

I didn't mind Daniel having girlfriends. Why would I? Lousy cheater. He could've apologized for that drunken one-night stand a thousand times and I wouldn't have taken him back. At least we didn't get married. Twenty-eight and divorced would've been devastating.

But Meghan really was a pain. The last time I went away, she borrowed my work shirts, leaving them in the hamper. If she laundered them I wouldn't have known, but I suppose that was her point. Who knows what else she takes. I resent doing inventory every time I enter and leave my house. That's how she earned her nickname "magpie." That and her high-pitched screeching, whether she's having sex or not. It's funny that she hasn't noticed I call her Mag. Maybe she thinks I have an impediment.

Mag and her big boobs (obviously fake), tiny frame, and bouncy blonde hair had sucked Daniel in. Lust bait. Her spa salary couldn't have been enough to pay for that boob job. Then again, maybe she saved enough money from living with her parents before she screwed her way into our house.

The only thing that made the situation tolerable was splitting expenses in high-priced Toronto area and a home for Pepper. Thankfully, Daniel did have a guilty streak and still loved me, so hopefully we can both bear it until I have enough for a condo next year.

I pulled into the driveway. Turned off the ignition. I was glad to get off the bike and straighten my sore back. I always looked forward to Pepper's greeting, his tail wagging like I'd been gone for ten years, but it also meant the end of my trip and the return to reality. Tomorrow, I'd be back at the casino listening to people complain about computer problems and missing my productivity targets because they complained at length. Not the greatest job, but okay for now.

"Honey, I'm home!" I bellowed as I opened the front door. This had been my greeting for five years, but now I said it as a joke. I ain't got no honey in this house.

"That you down there, Janelle?" Daniel asked. The sound of footsteps pattered down the stairs. "Welcome back," he said, giving me a big hug.

Daniel always hugged me for too long when Mag wasn't around, or at least he tried. I always liked his bear hugs. His broad shoulders. Even his little beer gut. He ate too much pub food and beer, but I never tired of his plain rugged face and brown, slightly curly hair. Daniel looked like he had just emerged from a lumberjack camp, which still appealed to me. Sometimes I let his hug go on longer if I was having a bad day, but today wasn't that day.

"Where's Mag?" I asked, stepping back from him.

"She's upstairs, napping," Daniel said, leaning in and rubbing my back. "Are you sore? Your back always gets so sore. How was the trip?"

I removed the motorcycle boots that had encased my feet like cement shoes on the long ride.

"It was great. Sunny the entire time. Nice, long meandering roads through the orchards. I loved it."

Daniel patted my hair down. "Helmet head," he said. "Did you like the book?"

"It was good, Daniel. Thanks for the loaner. Georgia O'Keefe was really quite something, wasn't she?"

17

"Yes, she certainly was. Strong and independent—a lot like you."

"I need a shower. Get the bugs out of my teeth."

Mag appeared at the top of the stairs, wearing her yellow negligee. Daniel brushed past me and planted himself beside her. "How are you, Meg? Did you have a nice sleep?"

"I did, Danny, thank you," she said, wrapping her arms around his neck and planting her head on his chest. Since when was he 'Danny'?

Attempting to slide past the glued bodies at the top of the stairs, I brushed up against Mag's back and she thrusted her body closer to Daniel's. "Oh, my goodness!" she said, her head spinning around in contrived shock. Ignoring her, I asked, "How's Pepper?"

"He's good. He's out back," Daniel said, his arms still wrapped around Mag.

I opened the patio doors and Pepper busted into the kitchen, his little legs taking flight. As I held him tightly, Pepper plastered my face with enthusiastic kisses. "You help me stay sane here," I whispered.

We both chose Pepper at the animal shelter. There he was, only six months old, wisps of white and blond fur framing his black eyes, barking at us, pawing at his cage door. I immediately fell in love with him and couldn't leave him there for one more night.

Pepper knew the routine when I came home. He raced upstairs after me and in one gigantic leap landed on my queen-size bed, barking riotously, and wagging his tail. I laughed. How I loved having my own fan club.

I dropped my keys into the empty Belgian chocolate box on my dresser, which Daniel gave me on Valentine's Day last year when he was between girlfriends. We'd flirted with the idea of becoming romantically involved again. Living in the same house brought that on pretty easily. Besides, it was difficult to erase our years together, starting in university. I still loved the jerk. Now I hung onto the memory of the Belgian chocolates, moistening my lips and swallowing an imaginary one.

My room seemed intact this time. The main items—the desk, beanbag chair, and paintings—were all there, as I expected them to be. Mag knew better than to touch my paintings that I had collected from my backpacking days in Europe and Central America.

My favorite shirts were still hanging in the closet with my shoes, not that I had a lot of either. Jeans or yoga pants and flip-flops were my regular uniform. Maybe Mag didn't do anything this time.

I really hated when she ransacked my room and took stuff. For a while I considered hand-combing my carpet upon exiting so it could capture any footprints and placing a yoga block tight against the back of the door. Shit, I had to stop watching crime shows. Maybe I was assigning more intelligence to her than she was actually capable of, but just the same, I wouldn't be surprised if she's scheming to have me kicked out.

"Why am I living with this?" I murmured, rubbing Pepper's belly. "To save money. To give us both a home."

In the bathroom, as usual, I threw the toothbrush in the garbage and opened a new one. If only Daniel would let me put a lock on my door.

In the mirror, I examined my sweaty hair pasted to my head, scraped off the little flies, and let the hitchhikers drop into the sink.

As the sounds of Mag's squeals began from Daniel's bedroom, I headed into the shower, and by the time I was cleaned and refreshed, the noises had stopped. Argh. I needed to live in the moment like my yoga teacher suggested.

"Focus on your breath, be aware of it going into your body, filling the space in your lungs, and reaching every cell in your body," my yoga teacher said. "Now breathe out, and with it all the negative emotions and feelings. Send them out of your body."

I inhaled and exhaled, observing the length of my breath, trying to lengthen my exhale. "Lengthening your exhale calms the nervous system," my yoga teacher said.

Breathing out all my negative experiences helped give me peace and made me feel more settled. The problem was my choice of men constantly restocked me with more negative emotions. I was self-replenishing that way.

Never had great luck with men. There'd been the Caribbean man who convinced me to spend most of my life savings on a botched real estate investment. It'd taken a lot of exhaling to dump my negative emotions over that one.

Then, the Indigenous man who'd taught me to live naturally and with Spirit but abruptly left when his wife sent me a text.

He's married. If you don't stop screwing him, I'll find you.

I didn't realize that screwing around was part of his "spiritual process." More exhaling.

Then the Christian man who refused to be intimate with me until "after marriage," which I suspected was just a coverup for sexual dysfunction. After months of living like a nun, I'd hit the road. Lots more exhaling.

And then of course there'd been Daniel. The relationship that was supposed to last a lifetime but ended in five years over a drunken one-night stand. But no final exhaling here. He was still around and I was in the worst situation of all. "Enough," I ordered myself, "Stop wallowing in self-pity."

I flipped open my Georgia O'Keefe book. Now, this was a woman worth admiring—leaving her philandering husband to enjoy an independent life in the desert with her friends and her art. I romanticized the notion and played with it, rolling it around in my mind. It could be just Pepper and me on the motorcycle, travelling in the southern United States in the winter, then cruising across Canada in the summer, doing the odd job for money.

They were at it again. Really, you guys, twice in one day? I started up my noise-cancelling headphones, an extravagance I allowed myself when Daniel started dating again.

Wouldn't it be satisfying for me to lend him the headphones one day, when my dry spell was over? I closed the O'Keefe book and scanned my bookshelf. Yoga books, chick lit, travel guides, and oh yes, *Best Laid Plans*—just to remind me I hadn't been laid for a while.

I heard them both right through my noise-cancelling headphones, which were apparently falsely advertised. I heard every bloody thing.

"Did they do this while I was away or is she being spiteful?" I asked Pepper. Pepper sat closer to me and licked my hand. "You do love me. I know that." I scratched his ears, and he put his head on my lap.

Pepper followed me downstairs. In the kitchen, my side of the fridge was bare except for some expired almond milk, kombucha, and tofu. Daniel's side was fully stocked with fresh fruit, milk, eggs, bacon, and sausages. I wished he wouldn't eat meat, but I never could get Daniel to change his food habits. His strawberries looked good, but I'd already eaten too much from his side of the fridge over the last while and didn't want to escalate the conflict.

"Come on, Pepper, let's go out," I said, patting him on the head.

I grabbed my suede walking shoes from the closet. They were scuffed on the outside and caked with mud on the bottom and sides. I always kept my favorite shoes clean. Dammit, that bitch did it again. I couldn't stand the thought of putting my feet in a place where she'd been.

Just then, my phone vibrated. It was a text from Yousef. He'd sent me an image of flowers. It was a bouquet of warmth on a truly shitty day. How sweet he was, this tall exotic stranger with an appealing accent—slightly British. He looked like a celebrity. I texted back.

Thanks for flowers. C U on my next trip to Kingston.

His response came right away.

You came to Kingston already. My turn if you don't mind.

He would drive to Toronto for dinner.

R U serious?

Yes.

I hesitated. I knew exactly where to take him. The belly dancing restaurant on Front Street. I wanted to go there for a long time but didn't have anybody to take.

Okay. Next Friday. Dinner.

He texted back.

Where can I pick you up?

Letting him pick me up at home in this threesome situation was a bad idea. Who knew what Mag would do? Besides, if this date bombed, I didn't want to rely on him to drive me home.

No. Coming from work.

I can pick you up at work.

He was so insistent, but so was I.

No. See you at the Moroccan restaurant on Front Street at 6 pm. I'll send the address.

Yousef didn't text back. Maybe he thought I was too blunt. Who knows what Egyptian men were like? Despite life's ups and downs, it brought new surprises. Life wasn't so bad after all.

CHAPTER 5

Today was the big date with Janelle. Canada certainly was an adventure. I never thought I'd be going on a date with a Canadian, nor would any of my friends.

I arrived in Toronto early to have plenty of time to check in to my hotel and walk the city streets to burn off some of my nervousness, but these six hours was too much time to wait and made me even more nervous, which, in turn, made me overthink.

In Egypt, most of the dates with my fiancée were in our families' homes with them hovering around us, cooking, laughing, and watching over our shy, tentative interactions.

A few times when we were able to pull ourselves away from the family dates, we walked through the old Cairo market, past the shopkeepers who tried to outshout and out-seduce each other in their attempts to lure us into their wares of lanterns, fabrics, and household goods.

"Come in!" one would shout. "Good prices here!"

"Tea for you?" another shouted, thrusting a paper cup at us. "Come in, have some tea, and take a look."

"Something nice for you," yet another said, coaxing my cousin with several bead necklaces draped over his arm. She laughed at his coaxing, both of us knowing that kindness aimed at your heart was the Egyptian way.

The shopkeepers helped me have a diversion from the awkwardness of making conversation with a fiancée who I hadn't even kissed but would be her husband upon her graduation from university. As each day went by, I became more nervous about the wedding night. Luckily, the entire thing fell apart before that over a bride price. Now, however, I was on my own.

I passed the Moroccan restaurant on Front Street, where I'd meet Janelle in a few hours, and continued to St. Lawrence Market. Maybe I could buy a gift here.

"Good morning, sir. How are you?" an older gentleman perhaps in his fifties with gray hair called out from the jewelry kiosk. The buttons of his plain dark blue dress shirt worked hard to keep his bursting belly caged in.

"Fine, thank you," I said, approaching his glass display counter.

"Looking for anything special?" The man leaned his belly over the counter, putting his hand under his chin.

Scanning his collection, the array of rings, necklaces, bracelets, and earrings shone back at me. "Something special, yes, but I'm not sure. I'm having a date tonight and was wondering if it's appropriate to buy her something?"

"I see. Women won't say no to jewelry," he said, waving his hand broadly over the collection. "That should surely brighten her day."

"It's the first date," I said, wondering if that should make a difference.

"Even better," the man said. "Make a great first impression and sweep her off her feet."

"Yes, I suppose so," I said, moving closer, running his words through my head. We don't say "sweep her off her feet" in Arabic, but maybe he means "fly from happiness." I would love to make Janelle fly from happiness.

"Fly from happiness," I said.

"That's it!" the man exclaimed. "Let her fly right up! What's your lady friend like?"

"She has brown hair. She rides a motorcycle and has big black boots and a black leather jacket. Beautiful green eyes."

The man paused. "Really!" he said, straightening himself fully upright, revealing more jewelry in the case. "What about this one?" he asked, reaching for a thin gold chain with a heart-shaped pendant.

"Too delicate," I said.

"Something tougher. More in line with the motorcycle," he agreed. "Maybe something in leather. Choker?"

"Choke her! Sir, I should think not!" I backed away from the display. What a mentally disturbed man.

The man stifled a laugh, covering his mouth. "Sir, I mean this," he said, picking up a thin black leather strap with a large silver heart fastened in the middle. "This is a gothic-style choker. There are adjustable snaps at the back for different neck sizes," he said. "It's not delicate, but beautiful just the same. A lady who rides a motorcycle would love this."

Still recovering from his choking comment, I said, "I'll keep that in mind. I'll think about it."

"We have many other beautiful pieces," he said. "We have a large selection. Biggest in St. Lawrence Market."

"Thank you, but I think I'll keep looking. Have a nice day, sir."

The man shrugged. "I hope you find what you're looking for."

Maybe what I already had for a gift was enough. Most people really liked Egyptian papyrus. I stepped outside of the market, the spring air cooling my face. I needed that. I cupped my hand around my neck, wiping off the nervous sweat. Across the street on the main level of the condo building was a barber shop. Not that I needed a haircut but freshening up might help calm my nerves. Besides, barbers all over the world were known as calming and good listeners.

Outside the barber shop, the sidewalk sign said: Why don't bearded men need vacuums? They already have crumb catchers.

Crumb catchers. More words to look up. Stepping inside, I was greeted by the familiar mixed smells of shaving soap, shampoo, and barbicide. The shop's six cutting chairs were filled with men draped in cloths, each having an attentive barber hovering over with scissors. One of the barbers turned toward me, his salt and pepper hair slicked back and longer than mine. "A cut for you, sir?"

"Yes, please."

"I'll be right with you. Just finishing up."

Within a few minutes, the barber dusted off the seat and draped a cloth over me. "Beautiful day outside," he said.

"Yes, it is," I said, remembering the cool air that hit my face. "I was in St. Lawrence Market."

"A great place. Any kind of food you want—Greek, Italian, Portuguese. Really shows off the diversity in this city. You want a regular cut? It seems like I don't need to take much off."

"Yes, a cut. I have a special date tonight, so I want to look good."

"I can do that for you, sir. I had a special date last week—my twenty-fifth wedding anniversary. One of the other fellas cut my hair," he said, retrieving his clipper. "A good haircut makes everybody shine on a big date with the wife."

"Thank you, but I'm not married," I said.

"Or for your girlfriend then," he said.

Girlfriend. Was Janelle a girlfriend or a date? Back home, I wouldn't call her my girlfriend. Nobody had a girlfriend, unless it was a secret.

"Not exactly a girlfriend," I said.

"Then a special friend," the barber said, winking at me.

Janelle wasn't a special friend, either. At least not in the way the barber was winking. A special friend might be somebody you secretly kissed when nobody could see—if you were lucky. I was so grateful I didn't have any secret kisses with my cousin because it would've been like kissing my sister. I'd never get engaged the Egyptian way again. One mistake in that direction was enough. I wanted a best friend, somebody to spend my life with.

"Maybe she's a special friend," I said. "Or a friend."

"Just as well. Why mess with labels? You like each other, then you like each other. That's it," he said, shaving the sides. "It's that simple."

"Yes, I agree," I said. "I do like her."

Janelle epitomizes Canada, rather than the corrupt, chaotic, and unpredictable Egypt.

"And if marriage comes, it comes," he said, buzzing the back of my neck. "If it ain't happening, that's okay, too. We were kind of forced to get married when we were young, but really, why bother?"

"I know what you mean," I said, running the family drama through my head.

"They want too much money," Dad moaned. "I'm already paying for the wedding and the marriage home."

"Her mother is very demanding about the wedding details," Mom agreed. "Too many fresh flowers everywhere—on the tables, at the entranceway, all those rose petals on the walkway. And then all the jewelry she wants. It's too much."

"Why can't she be happy living in 6ᵗʰ of October City, close to us?" Dad continued.

"Yes, they should be close to us," Mom said, even more adamant than Dad.

Listening to my parents moan was terrible enough. But then I'd hear it from my cousin, too.

"Please," she begged, "I want the wedding of my dreams, and I want to live in downtown Cairo near my family."

"We can go downtown anytime you like," I offered.

"I'll miss my family so much," she said. "As my husband, you should provide for me."

It was like the two families went to war, battling each other for more territory and control. I was caught in the middle of something I never wanted to be part of. I also knew what life would be like. As soon as we married, she'd stay home, clean the house, cook, do laundry, and have children while I carried the entire financial burden. We'd have our roles but not really be best friends.

No, I'd never try to marry a cousin again or anybody else my parents had chosen for me. "Sometimes marriage can be difficult," I said. "Families can be complicated."

"That's what I'm saying," the barber said, "If you enjoy each other's company then what little piece of paper will make a big difference?"

Yet in Egypt that little piece of paper meant everything to cement the everlasting bond between two families.

Some of my friends had Urfi marriages, but how could that be an option for me? I didn't want to buy a temporary marriage to get sex. Where was the love in that? It was a business transaction. Shaking my head, the barber moved his clipper away.

"Depends where you live, I suppose," I said.

"Well, sir," the barber said, applying the clipper to my neck, "You're right about that. A lot of strange things going on in the world."

"The world is different," I agreed.

26

"I'm a bit of a hippie at heart," the barber said. "Do what you want. Don't hurt other people. I mean, everybody knows what people do in hotel rooms. Affairs, or rendezvous or whatever you want to call it," he continued. "In my day, half of us signed in with fake names and paid in cash so we could carry on."

"Yes, of course," I said, but that would never happen in Egypt. All couples had to show their marriage license when checking into a hotel. Otherwise, if they booked two separate rooms and were caught together by the police in the night, they might be fined, go to jail, or both. It was too risky.

"Nowadays, you can't do that," the barber said. "They have cameras, make you book online. You have to try harder to cheat. But like I said, none of my business. I've been happily married for twenty-five years."

"I hope to be married someday," I said.

"You will be," the barber said, "But have fun before settling down. Take your time to find the right one."

"Sure," I said, wondering what that would feel like, making a decision of that magnitude alone without my family. Would I feel it in my heart or my head, or both?

"To start with, you're going to look like a million bucks for your lady friend. How'd you meet?"

"We met at a cafe. Actually, we met before that when she almost hit me with her motorcycle."

"And now you're going on a date? That's quite the story."

"I think so, too."

Yet it's a story to keep to myself for now.

The barber reached for the mirror. "How do you like the back and sides?"

"Good, all good. Thank you, sir." I didn't notice a difference from when I came in, but I enjoyed speaking with the barber.

"You can pay at the front. Good luck on your date tonight."

CHAPTER 6

At the Moroccan restaurant, perspiration assembled on my face. Not just because I was nervous about meeting Janelle. It was also Ramadan. I should've been at home fasting, like Mo, not meeting a single woman. Of course, my long trip to Toronto exempted me from fasting for today, thanks God, but I wasn't feeling very close to God right now. At least my excuse of taking pharmacy exam prep courses seemed plausible enough to Mo.

The décor reminded me of Moroccan design, every wall covered with silky-looking orange curtains. High-backed wooden chairs covered with orange fabric arranged around low wooden tables, compelling the kind of intimacy that food encourages. Antique-styled lamps on each table emitted a soft glow, while wall sconces reminded me of the ancient cobblestone alleys. Wooden room dividers adorned with Arabesque motifs separated spaces for privacy.

It'd been so long since I'd had dinner with a woman, alone, not since my engagement broke off. One benefit of dating your cousin was that you knew each other's family and could talk all night long. I ordered a Turkish coffee while I waited.

As I finished my second coffee, the hostess led Janelle in, past the clusters of people huddled around the tables, laughing and talking. She wasn't dressed up, but wearing her same black motorcycle jacket and boots, which I've come to know is her trademark style; nevertheless, she was as enchanting as the first time I met her. It might be too dramatic to say that my heart skipped a beat, but I think it did.

As I stood, Janelle lunged at me and wrapped her arms around my neck, pulling me downward. I froze. She was so open. I straightened myself and stepped back, breaking free.

After settling in and hearing about her day, I presented her with the Egyptian papyrus, a scene of Queen Nefertiti. She traced her fingers over King Tut's mother-in-law, captivated by the gold colors. We spoke about Egypt and I impressed her with some lesser-known facts: over one hundred pyramids, the female Pharoah Hatshepsut who disguised herself with a beard, and ancient Egyptians shaved their eyebrows when their cat died.

I ordered the Moroccan stew tagine, couscous, and salad for both of us. She ordered white wine and I ordered a ginger ale.

We chatted more about Egypt's history and politics. She seemed genuinely interested, so I kept talking and she kept drinking. One glass, then another.

"There are still so many antiquities," I said. "People dig in their backyards looking for them."

Janelle snorted. "That's what my dog does. Maybe now I know why he does it!"

I loved the way her eyes lit up. "Intelligent dog, but I'm sure he's been trained in a smart way by you."

Janelle tilted her head, her smiling eyes catching mine. "Do people find any treasures when they dig? Something fantastic, like gold?"

"I don't know, but many people try. They dig tunnels under their house," I said, admiring her green eyes. "Sometimes their house falls on them because they don't know how to create supports underground. Or they get too greedy and can't stop digging."

"That's sad," she said, "but so unbelievable to me at the same time."

Janelle raised her glass. "You're so sweet. Should we have a toast to new friends?"

So we were friends. That was a good start, and good to know. "To new friends," I said, touching her glass with mine.

The server brought a large platter of food for us. Janelle dove in, not holding back out of supposed politeness. She wasn't afraid to show any part of herself.

"Now you must eat all the food here," I teased, "Or like my uncle says, 'my daughters shall not get married.'"

"What does that mean?"

"It's a joke to tease guests, to encourage them to eat. Or if they don't have any daughters, they'll say, 'I swear I'll divorce my wife!'"

"I'm sure that some husbands would hope that would happen," she said coyly, serving herself more tagine. "I'll make sure your daughters get married."

What a healthy appetite she had. She'd fit right into the Middle East.

My phone rang, Mom's face lighting up the screen. She was going to ask how my Ramadan was going, and I guiltily silenced her. Instead, I explained to Janelle that Ramadan helps others to understand the pain of poverty. All the restaurants in Egypt would be closed during the day and it would be against the law to eat any food in public.

"Then why are you allowed to eat now? It's not sundown yet," Janelle asked.

"I'm exempt today because I travelled more than eighty kilometers."

"Lucky for the travelling salesman," she commented.

Mom called again, no doubt worried. At least Janelle wouldn't understand what I was saying. "Ahlan."

"Yousef, Mo said he isn't having Iftar with you tonight. What are you eating then?"

I couldn't lie to Mom, especially during Ramadan, but if she knew the truth, she'd run to Mo, then Mo would pressure me about what was going on. "I'm having Iftar with a friend."

"Who's that friend? What's his name?"

If I ended the call, I'd be lying the least amount possible. "Mom, I'm sorry, but it's so noisy in here. I'll call you back."

"Son, what's going on—"

"Mom, I'm so sorry. The noise is too much."

"I pray that God sends you the right way. We miss you here, son."

"I love you. *Salam*," I said, turning the phone off. I might have to deal with this later, but not tonight. "The pharmacy," I said, sighing. "They need me even on my day off."

"They call you in Arabic?" she asked, eyeing me.

"The pharmacy manager speaks Arabic," I said, not looking up.

All of a sudden, loud Arabic music began blasting through the speakers. Clapping to the beat started from the back of the restaurant and rolled towards us.

"Janelle, it's belly dancer time. Watch this," I said, pointing to the back.

The belly dancer wore a red bra top laden with gold beads and coins and a matching transparent red skirt. A long veil coiled loosely around her head and neck. Her long dark wavy hair moved as her hips shimmied to the beat.

She wove her way through the tables, circling her arms around and above her as she dropped, lifted, and twisted her hips, chest, and shoulders, smiling alluringly at men, some brave enough to insert rolled-up bills into her cleavage. The dancer moved through the room, her finger cymbals and the cheers and applause announcing her approach.

"She's good," I said, nodding my head. "She studied well."

Janelle tapped her hand on the table to the beat of the music. When the dancer came near, smiling at me, Janelle jumped up from her chair, jiggling to the beat. Janelle unrolled the veil from the dancer's neck and wrapped it around hers, letting it flow behind her. She moved her hips awkwardly from side to side, thrusting her pelvis toward the dancer in a jagged way.

"My first time!" Janelle called out to me. "Take pictures, Yousef!"

I nodded, horrified. Some people were pointing at Janelle and laughing. I hoped nobody knew she was with me.

As Janelle continued to advance on the belly dancer, the dancer moved further away, turning her back and focusing her attention on other customers. Janelle followed. Laughing. Twirling. Thrusting.

Suddenly, Janelle's veil wrapped around her boot like some wild snake that had trapped prey. She tripped and crashed into the belly dancer, falling to the floor and landing on top.

"Oh my god," screamed a customer.

Others pivoted around to gape at the spectacle. Janelle scrambled to stand up as the speakers continued to blast out the Arabic beat. The more she tried, the more entangled she became with the dancer. It looked like they were wrestling.

Rushing toward them, I hooked my hands under Janelle's armpits and yanked her up. I unwrapped the veil and, lowering my head, handed it back to the belly dancer, who glared at Janelle.

A black-suited beast, who was as tall as me but twice as wide, approached us from the back of the restaurant. I shoved a handful of bills into the belly dancer's hand, then slipped some to the man.

"My apologies. She gets so excited at your beautiful dancing." The dancer placed the money in the band of her skirt, then disappeared to the front of the restaurant.

The beast stood where he was. "We're leaving," I whispered to the man, placing another bill in his hand. "I'm very sorry."

He retreated somewhat as Janelle flopped into her chair.

"That was so much fun!" she howled. "It's hard to get those moves down. Talented hips. But these boots, they're so rigid. I need to take them off next time."

Next time? This was beyond humiliating. It wasn't even nine o'clock and we had to leave. I paid the bill and led Janelle outside.

"Yousef, thank you for such an amazing night. I loved it," she said. "It's so late right now. I should be going home."

"How? Not on your motorcycle?"

"I haven't figured that part out yet," she hesitated.

I didn't know what to do with her. I'd be so afraid if she went home at this hour.

"I'll get you a room in my hotel," I said. "Come this way."

***

Janelle protested the entire time to the hotel that she didn't want to have her own room but wanted to sleep with me. Inside, I smuggled her past the front desk to the elevator.

The elevator doors opened and another uniformed concierge stood inside. There was no getting past this one. I reached into my wallet and placed fifty dollars in the man's hand. He nodded and exited the elevator. "Have a nice evening," he said.

"Why did you do that?" Janelle asked.

"Privacy."

I'd never brought a woman back to my room before, and doing it during Ramadan was even more sinful. My stomach turned my dinner over a thousand times. When we reached the room, I quickly pulled Janelle in.

She threw off her boots and then jumped into the king-size bed. "This feels good," she said. She slithered her way to the top of the bed, slid under the sheets, then closed her eyes.

Janelle was more tired than I thought. Or was she trying to tell me something else, jumping into the bed like that? I definitely didn't want to harass her. Mo warned me that harassment was a big deal here. Was it still harassment when she came into *my* bed? Mo would never believe this, nor would I tell him. I couldn't tell anybody.

Janelle opened her eyes and let out a slow, long yawn. "So, here we are."

Suddenly, shyness tied my tongue. "Do you need to use the bathroom?" I asked.

"Yes," she said, rolling out of the bed. "Thanks."

I laid blankets on the floor beside the bed, removed my pants, and crawled underneath. As much as I wanted to have this beautiful woman, I didn't know what she wanted, so it was best not to try anything.

The bathroom door creaked open. "Hey," Janelle said, standing over me. "What are you doing? What's wrong with the bed?"

"You're in the bed."

"What's wrong with that?" she said, holding up her palms.

"I'm sorry, I can't do that," I said, talking to the ceiling.

"You can't do that … Oh, you're having problems?" Janelle sat on the edge of the bed. "It's okay. Sometimes that happens."

"Problems! I have no problems." I had respect for her, not problems. It's also Ramadan.

She nudged my legs with her feet. "There's pills for that."

"I know," I said, irritated. "I'm a pharmacist, remember?"

"So you are. Then why don't you take something?"

I couldn't believe I had to explain this to her, and now she was pressuring me. Continuing to talk to the ceiling, I said, "Janelle, we're not married."

Janelle covered her mouth, smothering her laugh. "Not married! Are you a virgin?"

"Me? Of course not!"

"Then why is your face getting red?" she said, pointing.

"Stop it! Just stop it!" I snapped.

"My friends won't believe this," Janelle muttered. "I can't believe this. What a twist of fate God has delivered to me," she said, raising her head and hands up to the ceiling.

"I'm sorry. It's different in Egypt. We need to get married. It's about your honor. It's also Ramadan."

"Sure, whatever. For your sake then, I'll give you one last dance." Janelle stood before me and slowly unbuttoned her black shirt, exposing her black lace bra and perfectly rounded breasts.

She was so sexual. How much I wanted to touch her. I diverted my eyes briefly, then was compelled to bring them back and trace the lines of her body. She unbuttoned her black pants and slid them down her hips, revealing her black lace panties and all her luscious curves.

"Now, for the finale! Don't look!" she sang out, unhooking her bra and throwing it on my face. Her sweet perfume enveloped me.

I did look. She was more beautiful naked than I could have imagined. My eyes couldn't stop following her body as she crawled into bed.

"You don't want any of this? Fine," she said, turning off the light beside her.

I was now in the dark with my sexual thoughts and the images of Janelle's beautiful body. They all slept naked. I knew that. Nudity was a normal part of life here. Even men in the locker room were naked in the West, walking around without modesty. Not even a towel.

"Good night, Janelle," I said, adjusting on the hard floor, pulling a blanket up to my chin. "I'm respecting you tonight," I said, raising my head to see her closed eyes and peaceful face through the moonlit streaks coming through the window, realizing at this point I was talking to myself. Janelle had already fallen asleep.

How tempted I was to slide into bed beside her and hold her tightly, feel her breasts against my body. But I was frozen, just like when I first met her at the café and couldn't move.

CHAPTER 7

Yousef towered over most of the other onlookers at the Kingston train station. I'd forgotten how tall he was. In his arms were a dozen red roses, and on his face, a warm, open smile. Clean-cut look paired with his athletic physique. He had a certain air about him, almost aristocracy, even in jeans and a polo shirt. Seeing him made me forget about our disastrous attempt at sex a few weeks ago.

We got into an Uber and wound our way through the Kingston streets to his home, going all over the map in conversation, from Beethoven to the Bee Gees to Egyptian jazz to literature greats like Margaret Atwood and Nagib Mahfuz. The Uber stopped in front of a large modern home, two small trees flanking the minivan in the driveway.

"This is your house?" I asked. "It's really nice."

"Not mine," he said quietly, "but where I am for now. I'm still deciding what part of the city to live in."

As we stepped out of the Uber and he led me to the side door, positioning me on his right side, he whispered, "There's an older couple living upstairs. We need to keep low voices. They sleep early."

"They're going to hear us on the driveway?" I whispered back.

The basement apartment was an open-concept design, the kitchen and living room all one room, and two more doors, presumably bedrooms, on the far end. The small kitchen was large enough for its small wooden table and two chairs, one of the chairs piled with books. In the living room was a large-screen television in front of a basic sofa, coffee table, and tall bookcase crammed with books. No weird shrines.

"Sorry for all these books here," Yousef said, moving the stack of books from the kitchen chair to the floor. "I'm studying for my pharmacy exams."

"It looks like a big process," I said, sitting at the table. "Those books are almost as tall as me."

Yousef laughed, a gentle, genuine laugh. He prepared a cheese platter in an intricate design with several types of cheese, green and black stuffed olives, and many types of crackers. It was like the cheese platters the VIPs had at the casino while the staff in the back office feasted on cheap sandwiches.

"Yousef," I asked, pointing to a family photo on the wall, "is this your family?"

He had the same oval eyes as the girl and the woman wearing a hijab, while similarly chiseled as the older man.

"Yes, my mother and father, and my sister," he said.

"Would they have a problem with me? You know, Canadian, not wearing a hijab?"

Yousef averted his glance. "Not at all. Janelle, you must be hungry."

We chowed down on the platter, him describing Halloumi versus Rumi, and me explaining what poutine is and why a cheese curd squeaks. Bringing me to his home was a big step in our relationship.

I was keen to learn more about his culture and family, but he seemed to want to skip over his broken engagement. Fair enough. I forgot to talk about my problematic threesome and cheating ex.

"I have a little gift for you," he said, handing me a small rectangular box.

Under the white tissue, a thin gold chain sparkled. "Yousef, it's beautiful."

"I noticed that you liked necklaces," he said, pointing to the chain on my neck.

"Can you help me put it on?" I asked, unclasping Daniel's necklace and stuffing it in my front pocket, also symbolically stuffing any memory of Daniel away. I turned, lifting up my hair and exposing my neck. He slipped the necklace around and secured it, his two hands smoothing it down. His fingers traced the form of my shoulders, lightly touching and lingering on my body. It was the first time he touched me. His breath quickened.

"So beautiful," I said, looking in the mirror on my phone.

I wrapped my arms around Yousef, squeezed tightly, holding on to him. His firm torso. He pulled away slightly, then kissed me lightly on the lips.

"You're welcome," he said.

Yousef gently pulled my hand, tugging me into the bedroom, checking with my wanting eyes. "Come," he said. "Tonight is our night."

The living room light streamed into the room as we kissed. A warm, soft kiss, but deeper and longer. I willingly succumbed to direction. Yousef wrapped his arms around me and silently laid me down on the bed, smiling as he kept an index finger to his closed lips.

He moved his hands over my body, tracing the lines and seams of my clothing from my collar to my pants. He lingered in tracing my breasts and pant zipper, teasing me, playing with my zipper, zipping it up and down, then lifting up my shirt, exposing my belly and kissing it all over, not saying a word the entire time. The passion was building inside of me.

"Yousef," I moaned.

"Without words," he said, pressing his lips to mine.

I pulled his shirt up from the bottom and tugged at it. Yousef smiled, then removed it. His bare, tanned chest, fully defined by muscle, aroused me even more. He tenderly removed my shirt, then cupped my breasts. I could feel his arousal as he pressed himself into me. Tonight is our night.

Yousef removed his pants, then put his hand on the button of my jeans. "Are you ready?" he asked.

I guided his fingers in unbuttoning and unzipping my jeans, slipping them off. Yousef smoothed his hands over my panties, reached behind, squeezed my buttocks, and climbed on top of me.

"I want to take our first night slow," he said. "I want you to always remember our first night."

"I am already," I said.

Each time he pressed his lips onto mine, he pressed his entire body into me, and I gasped. I wanted to scream. Are all Middle Eastern men like this? My gawd, I wanted more.

"You have so much lust bottled up," I said. "Let me help you release it."

"Shush," he warned, putting his finger to his lips before pressing down on my lips again. He fumbled with my bra and then slipped it off. I was completely primed and ready for him. My body was aching for him.

Then Yousef's phone buzzed. I glared at it, as if the phone had broken our momentum intentionally.

He ignored it, then slipped off my panties. I yanked off his underwear, and he climbed on top.

"Are you sure?" he asked, reaching for a condom.

"Oh, gawd, Yousef, just do it," I begged. "I can't wait anymore."

"Tonight is our night," he said. "I've wanted to do this for a long time."

His phone buzzed again. Yousef grunted, then reached for it.

"What?" I exclaimed, exasperated. "Yousef, forget it."

"I can't. Just a second." He read the text and then listened to his phone messages.

"Who is it? The pharmacy?"

Yousef paused. "The people upstairs. We're too loud."

"What are they talking about? Nothing's happened yet."

"I'm sorry, Janelle."

He climbed off me and sat on the bed. "They think I'm watching porn."

I pulled him towards me. "Buy them some bloody earplugs and let's keep going!"

"I'm sorry," he said, turning to face me. "They're old."

"And we're young, full of energy!"

"I'm sorry, Janelle. Maybe your house is better."

My house with my unhappy threesome. That wouldn't work. Better to have sex here.

"Yousef, you're a grown man who pays rent," I said. "Who can tell you not to have sex? I come all this way to see you, and two old people who still hear well are stopping us. This is ridiculous."

He shrugged his shoulders and turned out the light.

CHAPTER 8

Pepper awakened me with continuous licks. The skin on my right hand clearly had layers removed. I'd been dreaming about Yousef, except that it was a nightmare. He was hugging and squeezing me like a boa constrictor, squeezing the air right out of me. He kept slathering me with kisses on my face, lips, and neck while squeezing me even more. My rib cage was about to crack, and my eyes were on the verge of popping out.

Not that I didn't like the guy. I did. But he's just so … *intense.* Sending me texts every day since we crashed at the hotel. Endless romantic. But a gentleman. That's a nice quality.

Through the sliding doors, I could see Mag hovering over the blender, scraping down the sides of the glass. She dipped her finger into the concoction and sucked it. Well, that's a familiar pose for her. What was she making now? She better not have used my food to make it. I should find out.

"Hey Mag, what are you making?"

If it was any good, I planned to sneak some of it when she wasn't looking, as I usually did. Her food was much better than mine, which Pepper has even refused, that being one of the rare times he was irritating. Admittedly, blenders were too sophisticated for me.

"Something that you can't do, or won't," Mag said.

True, but still, she can't have the upper hand on anything.

"Oh, what's that?"

"You probably didn't even realize it's Daniel's birthday tomorrow. I'm making his favorite, a carrot cake."

How could I have forgotten! I'd remembered Daniel's birthday every year, even after we split up.

"I knew that it was his birthday," I lied. "I've known it for a lot longer than you have."

"Regardless, you're on the outside now."

That one hurt.

"You might want to try to add some dog food to that. It could improve the taste."

Mag blasted the blender. Not sure how, but I think she turned it up.

I was tired of these types of exchanges, but I couldn't resist them either. It was the usual daily sparring between us and almost a prerequisite to our days.

Being honest with myself, I couldn't stand that more of Mag was moving into the house. First her clothes, then her bed, because it was more "comfortable" than Daniel's, then her dresser, because she "needed" something for her things. Lastly, when I came back from Yousef's yesterday I saw Mag's sofa in the foyer waiting to be moved upstairs. As far as I was concerned, Mag was still a guest, and this whopping, full-sized sofa seemed to metaphorically take my place in the house.

I poured myself some coffee, paused, then filled it above the usual coffee line.

"Bad day?" Mag asked. "Or just a normal day?"

Mag poured the cake into the pan, then placed the empty jar in the sink. I stuck my finger in the bowl and withdrew a big clump of batter. It was pretty good. The cooked cake would be even better.

"That will be a yummy cake," I said. "Good job, Mag."

I even found excuses to say "Mag" just so I could get away with calling her a loud, squeaky thief without her knowing about it.

Mag kind of smiled, a proud smile.

I peered around Mag to the ingredients still left on the counter. "Mag, is that my soy butter? You buttered the pan with my soy butter?"

Mag stood in front of the soy butter, blocking my view. You'd think she was guarding the Crown. "I don't know. I got it from our side of the fridge."

I peered inside the fridge. "Yes, that's definitely my butter." I shook my almond milk carton. "Seems like there's less milk here. Did you steal some of that, too, Mag?"

"I didn't steal anything. Don't you care about Daniel's birthday?"

"Of course I do, but I can't afford to feed you and me."

I had no more time to argue. I had to get Daniel a birthday gift. He always remembered my birthday, even now. What would he really like that would outdo whatever Mag got him? She's baking a cake from scratch—he'll love that. How annoying.

I didn't know what he was reading these days, nor what he listened to. What else could I get him? Clothes … socks … shirts … maybe a dress shirt. No, that's not expensive enough. Maybe Mag already bought him that. A leather jacket? He'd love it. I ordered a bomber style, dark brown, short collar. It was so expensive but would completely flatten any kind of gift that Mag got him.

The one-day shipping would ensure that it arrived in time for his birthday tomorrow. On the card, I wrote: "Daniel, to my lifelong friend, I wish you an amazing birthday. I hope you like the gift. Love, Janelle."

Succulent smells of carrot cake filled the kitchen. Mag was now emptying it upside down onto the tea towel. It came out of the pan in one perfect piece.

"Don't eat any," she snapped as she left the kitchen.

I crept over to the cake. It really was a perfect-looking cake. It reminded me of the birthday cakes I tried to make for Daniel, except that my cakes always seemed to revolt against perfection, either being undercooked or lopsided or breaking apart as I tried to get them out of the pan. To Daniel's credit, he still ate every cake no matter how it turned out.

Birthdays were always special between us. I remembered the time he arranged a surprise party for me, secretly recruiting my friends to keep me busy and out of the house while he decorated the living room with balloons, streamers, and photos of us.

Then there was the time he whisked me away blindfolded to my favorite park in Quebec, Jacques Cartier National Park. We floated on inner tubes down the slow-moving meandering river that ran down the center of the park. We drifted down holding hands, taking in the rolling mountain view. At times, the turbulence of the rapids broke us apart, and we laughed and laughed without an end as we scurried toward each other again, frantically hand-paddling our way to join hands again.

There was also the time that I took him fishing. That's when I learned that Daniel had never caught a fish in his entire life, a fact that was conveniently omitted from all the interminable fishing stories he told but was painfully apparent after sitting in a boat for six hours without a bite. I'd assumed we were going to fry fish for dinner that night over the campfire, and we fought then guffawed about how we had to drive an hour into the next village to have fish burgers.

I held back tears. When it was good, it was perfect. Sometimes replaying the good memories was enough to make me believe I should allow Daniel back into my life again. I suspected Daniel would take me back if Mag was out of the way.

She just walked into everything I'd worked so hard to set up with Daniel. A relationship, friendship, house, and worst of all, a bed. Maybe I'd been too hasty in ending our relationship.

***

Daniel was in the kitchen, pouring a base layer of tomato sauce into the lasagna dish. I missed his cooking, which ended when we split up. "Hey Janelle, what are you up to this weekend?"

"Not much. I have this weekend off," I said, grabbing an apple from the fridge. "At least I hope. What are you and Mag up to?"

"Meghan is at her parents this weekend. I drove her to the bus," he said, "I'm making vegan lasagna. Remember when I used to make it for you?"

"Yum, yum," I said, exaggerating a lip lick. "It was delicious. Friday night lasagna and movie night."

"And what else?" Daniel pried, winking at me.

I laughed, dismissing his hint. "What are you using for the cheese?"

"The tofu kind," he said. "I got it from your side of the fridge. Is that okay?"

"Only if I get some lasagna," I said, chomping into my apple.

"Of course you do. I'm actually making it for us," he said. "I can't eat the whole pan by myself. Besides, I knew it was your weekend off."

Since when did he know when I was working? He had his head so far up Mag's butthole I didn't think he kept track of anything about me anymore.

Daniel added the lasagna layers of eggplant and tofu cheese, then a final layer of tomato sauce, careful to spread it to the edges over the eggplant so it didn't dry out. Just how I liked it.

"I'm surprised you're making it," I said. "You guys are dedicated carnivores, masticating on cow bones together like it was some noteworthy rite of life."

Daniel laughed but knew me enough to know that I was silently protesting the meat grease that hung in the air for hours. If I ran my finger down the walls in the kitchen, I'm sure I'd pick up residue. Not like this apple, I thought, as I placed the core in the garbage.

"Daniel," I said, picking up the bottle of red wine from behind him. "Are you having Châteauneuf-du-Pape tonight?"

It was so expensive I'd only ever had it when Daniel bought it. He made a lot more money as a technical writer than I did. "You do know that is one of my favorites."

"I wanted to splurge tonight," he said. "You can't have amazing food with a cheap bottle of wine, can you?"

"Actually, you could. Any kind of wine would go fine with that yummy dish."

"Would you like some?" he asked, not waiting for me to respond. He uncorked the bottle and poured me a glass.

Mag should go to her parents more often. "Such a rhetorical question. Great way to start the weekend."

Daniel poured himself a glass and raised it to me. "Cheers, Janelle. To a great evening."

"Cheers," I said, clanging glasses with him.

"Does it look terrific or what?" Daniel asked, showing his lasagna off to me and continuing to sprinkle tofu cheese on top.

"It really does. And I'm so hungry."

"I even got organic tomatoes," he said. "You need to do it right, if you do it at all."

My eyebrows jumped into my hairline. He really did know how to do it right.

"I'm surprised you remembered."

"Janelle, I remember so much about you ... and us. I don't know why it surprises you. Janelle, sometimes I feel like we're still together." He tried to grab my eyes with his gaze, but I looked away. Still together, sure, except that Mag lives here.

I sipped my wine.

"Meghan has a hard time with us still living together, I'm sure you've noticed. I know Meghan can be difficult sometimes," he said, topping my wine up.

"Sometimes I want to let Pepper lick her leftovers in the fridge," I said.

"Those are my leftovers, too, Miss Janelle," he said, putting an arm around my shoulder. "You know, she does fill a void in my life. You understand that, don't you?"

Certainly I did. I'd moved on ten times more than Daniel, even if he never knew it. My romantic life wasn't his concern. Besides, he might get upset that he was "ten or so boyfriends ago" and not be willing to share the house until I had enough money for a condo.

"Mag seems to be good for you for now. Who knows how it'll turn out? Maybe you'll get married."

"I don't know about that," he said, sipping his wine. "To be honest, we fight quite a bit. I don't know if you hear us."

"I assumed all that noise was you hitting a home run."

"Touché," he said, clanging glasses. "She's applying a lot of pressure to get married."

"After six months?" If they got married, he'd definitely want to buy me out.

"But she's also not contributing much because she spends all her money on makeup and clothes. So, it puts a lot of pressure on me."

Daniel took a big gulp of wine. "The more I know her, the more I think about our relationship instead. We had some good times, Janelle. A lot of them."

I could feel Daniel's eyes trying to connect with me, but I didn't look up. It was best for me if he still hung onto nostalgia, that he didn't move on, even if I already had.

"Are you seeing anybody?" he asked.

"It sounds like you need some more time," I said, ignoring his question.

Actually, I was the person who needed more time. I hoped Daniel would maintain the status quo for one more year. "No sense in making any drastic changes, is there, Daniel?"

"Janelle, when we were together, it's not something you forget. We both made mistakes. We're only human."

As long as he was still regretful about our relationship, he wouldn't want to buy me out. God knows I could never live with my family and their chaos.

"You're right, Daniel. It's hard to forget our relationship. We were really young, weren't we?"

"That's what I'm saying. I think we both learned a lot more about each other."

"Daniel, for tonight, why don't we have this wonderful evening with each other?" I suggested. "You've made this beautiful lasagna and you got my favorite wine. I appreciate this so much. It's very thoughtful."

I reached my arms around his neck and squeezed him hard, holding onto him. He didn't pull away.

When the oven timer buzzed, Daniel took the steaming, bubbling dish out of the oven, then served two huge servings for each of us. I immediately stabbed a piece of eggplant, swirled it in the tofu cheese and tomato mix, blew on it, then plunged it into my mouth. "Daniel, this is outstanding."

"You like it?"

"I love it."

We devoured the lasagna, overstuffing ourselves like raccoons in a garbage bin, reminiscing about the fun we had. Daniel was still one of my best friends. When we finished, he put our plates into the dishwasher and declared, "I have a special surprise for dessert."

"What?"

Daniel retrieved a bag from the closet. "It's your favorite."

"You didn't."

"I did."

"I can't believe you bought Belgian chocolates!" I screamed, jumping up from the table and hugging him.

"Believe it," he said, hugging me even tighter.

I gently broke free from his hug. I knew where he thought the Belgian chocolates were heading, and he'd have to wait until Mag got back to get laid. My phone began beeping, which gave me the excuse I needed to get away from him. "Daniel, I'm sorry, but I hear my phone beeping. I'm waiting for an important text from my boss," I said, running into the kitchen.

Yousef texted.

Janelle, I hope that you're having a wonderful weekend.

I texted back.

U2.

He texted again.

Can I call you?

Before I responded, my phone rang. "I'm sorry," I said, poking my head out of the kitchen and pointing at my phone. "I have to take this. It's work. Thank you so much for dinner. I'll come down later for the chocolates."

Daniel's face fell as if he'd heard devastating news. As I climbed the stairs to my room, Yousef asked, "Janelle, who are you talking to?"

"My brother."

"Say hello to him for me. I hope to meet him someday."

"Sure, I will. He'd really like to meet you, also."

CHAPTER 9

I folded my nicest hijab around my face, covered my neck, and pinned it into place. As per usual, my hijab matched my blue blouse and jeans. My hijab was a statement to others that God was almighty, gracious, and good, and I observed Him, but I must admit on Cairo's thirty-degree days like today, I couldn't wait until I returned home and stripped it off my head like a man discards his tie at the end of the day.

I don't know why Rasha insisted that I had to go to Yousef's parents' house to get his pharmacy documents: "Sarah, you must go! I expect this of you as your older sister. Yousef's mom needs to hand you the documents personally."

Inside, I was groaning but outside of course I respected her. Why couldn't they send the documents in a taxi? Maybe they were sensitive documents? Now I had to cross Cairo's crazy traffic in this sweltering heat when all I wanted to do was stay home. After all, it was Ramadan, and I'd be so hungry and thirsty by sundown that I'd devour everything in front of me. I was already boiling underneath this hijab and the thought of going several more hours without water made me thirstier. At least Rasha got an Uber for me. I took the elevator downstairs and the driver was already there.

He called out of his window, "Good morning. Are you Sarah Sayed?"

"Salam, yes, I am," I confirmed, getting in the back seat and closing the door. "Going to 6th of October City."

The car's air conditioning was like stepping into a fridge and was a nice reprieve from the heat. I delayed taking this trip for Rasha, partly because I was avoiding the hour-long journey in a microbus across the city.

"Hire a private taxi," Rasha urged. "It's going to be too hot for you to travel on the microbus. Don't you want to arrive relaxed and smelling good?"

"How would I hire a taxi?" I asked. Rasha then transferred me the money right away. Ever since Rasha moved to Canada, she's been more successful at getting deeper into Mo's pockets.

The Uber wound its way along the Ring Road past the Pyramids that seemed to sit patiently amidst the traffic mayhem, hundreds of microbuses crammed onto the highway. Unlike the microbus, I had a seat to myself today. How uncomfortable it would have been—greedy drivers stuffing customers in to get more fares, men sitting beside me with barely a thumb between us, then others hanging on the outside as the microbus lived in dangerous traffic. These 1970s Volkswagen vans told their own life stories, their bodies replete with the typical dents, dings, and scrapes from the Cairo traffic bumping up against them.

The Uber driver competed for space on the freeway with the microbuses, cars, donkey carts, and scooters that filled the Cairo air with its usual sense of systemized chaos and pollution. Finally, we entered 6th of October City.

The Uber drove past some of the largest houses I've ever seen, painted white or pastel pink, yellow, or green, not the dull, plain unpainted gray of my apartment building. These families would have had the entire two-story house and extensive grounds to themselves, unlike my family and our tiny apartment in the twenty-story building. The driver stopped in front of large iron gates that protected a gated community. I dropped a tip into his hand and stepped out.

Yousef lived here? Rasha said he was wealthy, but a gated community? I've only ever imagined what lies behind the gates. These rich people were insulated from mingling with the real Cairo, living in their oasis in the chaos.

The security guard stepped outside his station. "Good day, Sir," I said. "I'm here to see Madam Huda El Sherif."

He signed me in the logbook, photocopied my identification, and buzzed me into the compound. I sauntered, taking in the beautiful gardens and attempting to cool myself under the giant palm trees. It was so different from the city of cement.

The large red roses were lush, incontrovertibly watered regularly in this desert heat. Even the air was better in the compound, without the grit and exhaust of daily life, and I savored the feel and taste of it.

The sports club behind the two-story Spanish-style terracotta villas assumedly contained the swimming pools, tennis courts, and maybe a golf course. Wouldn't it be nice to jump into the pool today, at least dip my feet to cool down? Have a life of such affluence, with drivers, house staff, and cooks? No rusty cars with dents here, I noted, passing a Porsche that was resting under a palm tree. Yousef's parents definitely had the means to have easily sent the package, so why did Rasha insist for so long that I come pick it up personally?

I pressed the intercom button at their house. "Good morning, this is Sarah. I'm here to see Madam Huda, please."

The door opened, and a young Filipino woman smiled. "Good afternoon, Sarah. The Madam is ready for you in the salon." She piloted me inside, past marble statues, Aubusson tapestries, European artwork in thick gold ornate frames, and into an antique Baroque chair. The chair probably cost more than my annual salary. My humble self shouldn't even be sitting in a chair like this. This house was like a museum.

It'd been years since I saw the Madam. She was always regarded as such a beautiful woman, and today was no different. She entered unhurriedly, as if making an entrance onto the stage, her long silk gold and brown galabeya that covered her down to her ankles flowing into the room with her. Her matching hijab framed a face that lacked the typical stress marks of a long, hard life found on many Egyptian women in their late fifties, including my mom. She wore a thick gold necklace with diamonds so large it would weigh even a strong person down. The housekeeper stood attentively by, carefully watching her every step.

The Madam's graceful, movie-star entrance was in such contrast to my plain appearance, hijab and jeans. Rasha told me to wear my best dress, and now I knew why. I tucked my feet under the chair to hide my plain shoes, covered with the grime of Cairo, and moved my handbag to the side of the chair, but she'd already spotted the nondescript department store piece. I immediately stood up, gently shaking her hand and kissing her cheek.

"Hello, Sarah, my dear. Thank you for coming. How you've grown up to be such a beautiful woman! When I saw you last at Rasha's wedding, you were still a child!"

"It's a pleasure to see you again, Madam," I said. "You're in a beautiful new home now."

"Yes, for a few years we've been here," Madam said. "We enjoy it." Madam sat on the Baroque-styled sofa and gestured for me to sit down. "It's so kind of you to offer to bring these documents to Yousef. Your sister has said so many kind words about you."

Madam pointed at the incense burner on the table in front of me. The housekeeper obliged and lit the stick, frankincense suffusing into the air. Even their incense was better smelling than what we had.

"It's a pleasure," I said.

"I told Rasha that we'd send the driver to you but she insisted that you'd pick it up," Madam said. "As far as I recall, you used to live in Imbaba."

"We're still there," I said. "My father inherited that apartment. It used to be a nice neighborhood but it changed, like many places and things in Egypt, as you can imagine."

"I hear you. Even long before your family, that area used to be a camel market, but as you rightly put it, things have changed," Madam said. "That's why I insisted to buy a house in a gated community this time to avoid such unplanned growth. Tell me about yourself, dear. Are you still in school?"

"I finished a degree in business seven years ago. I'm working as a secretary for now."

"As Rasha said. So you're intelligent as well as beautiful. And a hard worker. These are wonderful qualities to have."

"Thank you. You're very kind," I nodded.

"And thank you again for bringing this package to Yousef. My son is very good, but I feel that he's so lonely right now. He misses his family, especially his mom." Madam placed her hand on her heart. "You know how men miss their mothers, no matter how old they are."

"Yes, I really do understand," I said. "It must be very difficult for him."

"Of course, I'd love for him to come back home. Our daughter will marry and go with her husband one day. What'll become of this beautiful home and the family business?"

Madam waved her arms around in broad sweeping gestures at her grand home, then pointed to the life-size painting of a man behind her. His hair was silver and cut short, and he wore a dark suit and tie. "Yousef's dad," she said. "Mr. Fahmy El Sherif. He inherited the export business from his dad and greatly expanded it. He's a great man."

"I remember him, even when I was small," I said. "Your beautiful home is obviously the result of a very successful business. It'd certainly be a shame if your son remains in Canada, wouldn't it?"

"He will return, God willing. Only God can stir the hearts in the right way, dear. If it's God's will, it shall happen. Of course, I worry about what he's being exposed to, the Western ways. You understand, don't you?"

"Of course, I certainly do," I said. "God is great. Madam, I'm so sorry, I appreciate meeting you, but I prefer to arrive home in the daylight to prepare for the food tonight. Do you have the package for Yousef?"

"Yes, of course," she jerked her head at the housekeeper, who immediately disappeared into another room.

"Yousef requested some documents for his pharmacy recertification," Madam said. "Would it be all right with you if I also send some dessert? It's Yousef's favorite, my konafa."

"No problem at all," I said. "Madam, that is one of my favorites as well. I found the secret to good konafa is to use quality ingredients and real butter, not ghee."

"My dear, Sarah!" she said. "I agree with you. And let's not forget that the sugar syrup should be cold when drizzling on the hot konafa, right?"

"Absolutely," I said, emphatically. Only good cooks know this secret.

"Believe this," Madam said, pointing her finger in the air, "it was my konafa that captured the stomach of my husband and then his heart. He couldn't stay one more minute away from me after tasting it."

Madam smiled in self-satisfaction at her conquest. A good Egyptian woman was all about cooking. Even with beauty, if an Egyptian woman couldn't cook, she couldn't keep a hold on her husband nor get approval from her mother-in-law.

"My mom taught me how to cook very well, Madam," I said. "I love cooking."

Madam eyed me intently, then smiled. Cooking was one attribute that didn't break along class lines; even the poorest of women could satisfy a man's stomach. All a woman needed was a stove and a pot, and to prepare the food with love.

I accepted the large envelope and tray of konafa from the housekeeper. "Thank you. The konafa will still be nice and fresh when I arrive in Canada."

"Yes, Mo and Rasha tell me that you're going to help Rasha with her baby for a while."

"I'll help her for the first few months, when she really needs it. I can stay up to six months on the tourist visa."

"Six months should be enough time," Madam mumbled, almost too quiet for me to hear. "What a delightful young woman you are, like Rasha said. Helpful, beautiful, and most of all, a fantastic cook."

I smiled again. "Thanks Madam. It's time for me to go."

"Yes, you need to drive back in the daylight. That's wise, Sarah."

"I don't drive, Madam," I said, casting my eyes to the marble floor.

"Then your driver is coming for you? I'm so sorry, but if I knew I would've sent the package with our driver to you."

"I took an Uber," I said. "It's waiting for me."

"I see. Well, I'm sure we'll meet again soon. Thank you for coming."

I gathered the package and konafa, kissed Madam on the cheek and shook her hand. I only had a few more hours to get back to Imbaba before the sun went down, and before the street dogs packed together and took over the poorly lit streets.

Walking out of the compound, I lingered in the luscious gardens and rose bushes for as long as possible before returning to my cement jungle neighborhood. It'd be nice to be this wealthy, but I wasn't resentful against Yousef's family, for all people are equal in the eyes of God on judgment day.

CHAPTER 10

Canada was so unknown to me. I only knew it was big and cold, with huge distances between cities. But when Rasha asked me to help her with the new baby, of course I'd come. I was first struck by how all the drivers stayed in their own lanes on the highway, then at how huge their house was.

As I sat at the kitchen table, Rasha prepared the glasses, each with a sprig of fresh mint and teabag, then poured the boiling water.

I pointed to my glass. "It's the right color. Canada didn't change that."

Rasha laughed and hugged me. "Not too strong and not too weak. The perfect red color. I'm so glad you're here. I missed you so much." Rasha hugged me again.

Rasha was enthralled at the latest news in the family and the neighborhood, the typical stories that lubricated the wheels of Egyptian society. The list was always the same. Who was sick. Who died. Who got engaged. Whose engagement fell apart. Who got married. Whose wedding was extravagant and whose wasn't. Who got divorced. Who was pregnant. Who had a baby. What the latest government scandal was. Who was arrested by the police and disappeared. Who got run over by a camel and was now recuperating. She expressed surprise, shock, joy, and bewilderment to each of my stories. I continued.

"You remember our old neighbor, the one who died last year? The one who used to give us candy when we were kids and his wife cleaned houses?"

"Of course, I remember him, may his soul rest in peace."

"His wife just told Mom that when she was at her husband's funeral, there was a woman across from her crying and wearing black. She thought, 'Who was that woman who was crying uncontrollably?' Even more than her. A relative she never met?'" I said, sipping my tea. "You know who it was?"

"I can't even guess," Rasha said.

"His second wife!"

"What! His second wife! And the first wife never knew about her!"

I laughed. "Our neighbor was laughing when she told Mom, and Mom was laughing when she told me."

Rasha laughed, holding her belly. "Time heals so much. Humor heals everything," she said. "If you live in Egypt, you definitely need a sense of humor. Oh, Sarah, the stories of our people," she said, shaking her head. "I know you must be so exhausted from the flight."

My hands propped up my head. "My eyelids feel like a heavy weight is sitting on them. I can't believe I forgot to bring the konafa."

"Jet lag will take a few days," she said. "Try not to go to sleep until bedtime, and the next day you will wake up fresh and rested. Let me help you make a new konafa," she said, leaning forward with her finger on her lips, "Yousef doesn't need to know."

"Rasha, you've always been the better cook. You could do this with your eyes closed. Like my eyes right now," I teased.

"You're also a wonderful cook, Sarah. You're just tired right now."

She heated the milk and sugar over the stove until the sugar dissolved, then added the cornstarch, constantly stirring to avoid the lumps, and removed the mixture from the heat.

"I could use some more tea," I said. "Do you mind if I make some more?"

"My kitchen is your kitchen," she said, straining the cream filling in the sink.

"Yousef's mother is really proud of her konafa," I said, watching the liquid disappear from the kitchen sink. "I feel so bad that I forgot it."

"Please don't worry," Rasha said. "Everything will be fine. Did she use butter or ghee?"

"Butter. Only butter," I said. "She insisted."

"Yousef won't taste the difference, you'll see," Rasha said. "He'll think he's eating from his mom's hands. So you met his mother? How did that go? I heard their home was beautiful."

"I never wanted to leave the gates. I thought, how could I stay here forever, watching these beautiful gardens and pools every day?"

"It'd be nice, definitely, to marry into a family like that," Rasha said. "Who knows? You already know him, and you're a great cook. He's the right age at thirty-three."

"And I'm a bit old, at thirty-one, I know, sister."

"Come on, Sarah, I didn't say that," Rasha said. "But I was married much younger than you. You haven't found the right man yet."

"Where would I find him? Where has he been hiding?" I laughed.

"Who knows … maybe underneath us," Rasha said.

"Rasha, you're so funny. It's like you're planning my wedding already," I said, patting her shoulder.

"Keep sharpening your cooking skills, Sarah. Here, take a look."

As I looked on, Rasha shredded the phyllo dough into long strands, mixed it with the sugar and melted butter, and pressed it into a pan. "You need to press the dough in so it's even throughout," she said. Rasha added the cream filling on top, then the rest of the dough to seal the dish.

"The final secret is to put some more butter on top. It'll melt in and be absolutely delicious," she said.

"Rasha, this is already smelling good," I said. "Being part of his family would be nicer than spending my life as a secretary in Cairo. Would Yousef have a house like this when he gets his pharmacy license?"

"He surely should. Most definitely," Rasha said.

"What's Canada really like?"

"Canada is so different from Egypt," Rasha said. "But Kingston is home. It's the best place for our children."

Rasha continued. "I couldn't imagine what kind of future I would have had had we ended up somewhere else, where I wasn't allowed to leave the house without Mo's permission, couldn't drive, and had to keep my entire face fully covered."

Canada is free. We all knew that. "Do the kids still go to the Islamic school?"

"Every Saturday. And you can get Arabic groceries here, too, in the main grocery stores. For the special food we drive to Ottawa once a month."

"Halal in Kingston? That gives me a lot of comfort."

"Now Sarah, can you put this in the oven?" Rasha asked, passing me the konafa. If I helped even slightly, Rasha could assign me credit for the dish in front of Yousef. I might be the younger sister, but I knew when my sister was matchmaking. I slid it into the oven.

"Let's keep an eye on it," Rasha said, "so it doesn't get too brown. I'll finish making the sugar syrup and we'll drizzle it all over when it comes out."

She turned on the oven light, and we crouched down, peering into the oven through the glass window.

"This is like watching a television show, isn't it?" Rasha suggested, patting me on the back.

"Rasha, you know what to do," I said, smiling into the oven door. "About everything. You've always been the smarter sister."

"And you the prettier one," she said. "God gave us each something to get a husband. It only needs about forty minutes in this oven. Let's sit and have some more tea."

Rasha made me some more tea and garnished it with another piece of fresh mint. "You know what's different from Egypt? All the rights women get here."

"What do you mean?" I asked, sipping her tea.

"In marriage," she said. "I own fifty percent of this house."

I put down my glass. "How is that possible?"

"That's the way the marriage laws work here. You own fifty percent of everything."

"Rasha, this beautiful house. You stay home, take care of the family, and own part of the house yourself?" I examined the floor, cupboards, and even the light fixtures. "Not in my entire life would we ever own a house in Cairo."

"Never, I agree. In Egypt, you need that," Rasha said, pointing to my gold necklace.

I touched my chain. "Of course we do. Gold is the only financial reserve that we have if our husbands leave us."

"In Canada, you're entitled to half of everything," Rasha said. "Not that I have any problems with Mo, but if he wasn't nice to me, I could make a complaint against him. I have rights here."

"That sounds like a dream," I said. "What can we do in Egypt with a cruel husband? Nothing."

"Unless we had a police officer in the family," she said. "Right?"

"So true, Rasha. Every woman needs one of those in the bloodline."

When the konafa was done, Rasha took it out of the oven and displayed the dish. "Look at the perfect brown on top."

"That does look like his mom's konafa," I said. "Wonderful job, Rasha."

"We made it together, but you put it in the oven," she winked. "That was the special touch."

"Rasha, you're too much," I laughed.

"When the syrup is cold enough, drizzle every part of it, let it soak in nicely. No man can resist this," she said. "Now, bathe and wear your best galabeya and perfume. We'll have a quick dinner and then Yousef will come up for tea."

Sister knows best.

CHAPTER 11

As usual, I was lured up from the basement by the cooking aroma. Rasha had been cooking again, and the sweet smells of her food seeped under the door and floated downstairs. I knocked gently, and Mo opened the door. "Hey, Yousef. Come on in." Mo gave me a quick hug, no kissing on the cheek like we used to do back in Egypt.

"What's up, Mo! Where are the kids?"

"Playing upstairs," Mo said.

Mo led me into the living room, where Rasha was sitting. She struggled to rise from the sofa.

"Rasha, please," I said, motioning with my hands to stay seated. "Let me come to you."

"Yousef, you're always the gentleman."

"How are you today?" I shook Rasha's hand.

"I'm fine. My baby is coming soon," Rasha said. "And my sister is already here. "We just picked her up from the airport today."

"Sarah? That's wonderful news," I said. "I haven't seen her since your wedding."

Rasha turned her head toward the kitchen. "Sarah!" Rasha called out, "Yousef is here."

"When she was just a girl," Rasha said.

Within a few minutes, Sarah emerged from the kitchen with a silver tray, carrying a tea urn and glasses. She wore a beautiful red and orange galabeya. It was simple in design, like the ones middle-class women wore, but nonetheless, beautiful. I could easily see how curvy she was underneath. The tray reflected the light around her, making her skin appear lighter and brighter.

"You remember my lovely sister. See how beautiful she is?" Rasha asked.

Sarah placed the tray down and smiled shyly at me. She took a small step toward me, her perfume drifting. The sweet smell of Arabic perfume enticed me.

I waited for Sarah to extend her hand, which she did reluctantly after taking silent approval from Rasha, who nodded. Sarah's clasp was soft and only seconds long, unlike Janelle's handshake that almost tore my rotator cuff.

"It's a pleasure to meet you again, Sarah. Thank you so much for bringing the documents with you. You helped me with a great burden. Thank you so much."

The kohl eyeliner emphasized her beautiful eyes. She blushed, moving her eyes away from me to the tea urn. I also averted my eyes. I couldn't be so impolite.

"You're most welcome. Your mother is a lovely lady and it was a pleasure to do this for you. And for her," Sarah said. "Would everybody like some tea?"

Sarah poured the tea into four glasses and handed one to each of us. She then retrieved an envelope from the kitchen.

"Your pharmacy documents," she said, handing them to me.

"Thank you so much, Sarah. I really appreciate that you brought this for me."

"You're most welcome," she said.

"Yousef," Rasha said, "Your Mom also sent some konafa."

"My Mom's konafa! Please, let's all have some. She makes the best konafa. You have to try Mom's konafa," I said.

"I'll get it," Sarah said, disappearing into the kitchen.

"I think it travelled well," Rasha said, smiling.

Sarah brought out the konafa and serving dishes and placed them on the table. "Freshly heated in the oven."

Sarah served the konafa onto four plates, and I immediately pushed a big forkful into my mouth. "That perfect crunch," I said, scooping another piece into my mouth. "This is definitely my mother's konafa. Makes me miss Egypt."

I shoved into my mouth several more bites of konafa before the others had even picked up their forks. How could I be so rude? I guess I missed Mom more than I thought. Mo laughed heartily, and Rasha and Sarah giggled. They all looked at each other, then erupted into laughter again.

I put down my fork. "What are you all laughing at?"

"It was a busy day for Sarah, and she almost missed the plane," Mo said.

"Okay..." I said.

"She had to rush to the airport and forgot your mom's konafa."

"Then what's this?" I asked.

"We've one wonderful sister in Sarah," Rasha interjected. "Immediately off the flight, hungry and very tired, she made a new konafa the same way your mom made it. I couldn't believe it when she did that. I remember coming off an Egypt Air flight and barely keeping my eyes open for days."

"I hope you liked it," Sarah said. "Your Mom and I talked about konafa and we realized that we made it the same way."

"It tasted just like Mom's konafa," I said. "It was absolutely delicious. But don't tell her I said that."

"Sarah will be here for a while," Rasha said. "She loves to cook."

"I can't say no to that," I said. "If it's not a bother to you. The only thing I can cook is microwaved falafels." Having real Egyptian food would give me one of the missing ingredients in my life that I missed and so badly craved.

"Not a bother at all," Rasha said, glancing at Sarah.

"No bother," Sarah said. "I love to cook. I just don't have a lot of people to cook for."

While my sister was taught to cook, I was banned from the kitchen like all men. Every time I approached the kitchen door, the family staff would ask me what I needed.

"Sarah has no other commitments," Rasha broke in. "That's why we're lucky as she can stay with us a long time. Yousef, another piece?"

"I can't refuse," I said, presenting my plate to Sarah. "What are you doing in Cairo?"

"I'm a secretary in a pharmaceutical company," she said.

"Sarah finished her business degree from Cairo University," Rasha said. "She was near the top of her class."

"I see," I said. "Congratulations! That's a great--"

"Did you ever think a woman so smart would be a cook like that? Women like this are a rare find, who take care of their men and families, and work if the man has no objections," Rasha continued.

Rasha was so traditional, sometimes I hardly knew what to say to her. Sarah broke the silence.

"What do you like about Canada, Yousef?" Sarah asked.

"Many things, but mostly the chance to be treated like a human being with rights," I said. "Here, you can speak your mind without fear of detention or harassment, or anything."

"It's certainly important to have that. A country isn't a country without human rights, and it affects the country's economic development. Do you like the people as well?" she asked.

"Yes, the people are kind," I said, "but I do miss the café culture of Cairo. Down every little alley, the coffee shops and backgammon games. People know each other."

I really missed the social interactions in Egypt, the flow of conversation, the way that one person picked up where the other one left off, trying to outdo each other with their stories. All of their elaborations, which we knew, of course, was exaggeration to add life to the conversation. I missed their generous, warm greetings.

"Warm hearts always shine through," I said. "Here there are a lot of warm hearts, even in the crazy cold weather."

"The weather would be hard for me to get used to," she said. "The snow."

"I haven't seen real winter yet," I said. "I'll let you know how that goes."

We all laughed.

"It's fine," Rasha added. "You get used to it quite quickly."

"Now I'm also learning English," I said. "Some of the terminology in the pharmacy is different, and the street slang is hard to pick up sometimes."

The truth was, I missed the way the conversational poetry of Arabic, the way it wrapped itself around your soul. A story that might take two minutes in "Canadian" would take twenty minutes in "Egyptian," as the speaker embellishes with excess words and detail to make the story more palatable to the ear and the heart. Conversation was about the soul, not just the words. "I'm learning a lot every day."

"I heard that Canada isn't very religious. So many nonbelievers live here," Sarah said.

"I don't know about that," I said. "Because I don't know many Canadians yet, but religion isn't talked about, and it doesn't form the government and the law like in Egypt. I like this about Canada a lot."

"It's how a country should be," Sarah agreed, glancing at her sister.

"Yes, I think so," I said, "Otherwise, only the dominant group of people feel welcome."

"It shouldn't be that way at all," Sarah said.

"What if—" Mo interrupted. Rasha reached over and patted his leg.

"All people should have religious freedom," Sarah continued. "To practice what they believe in."

"That's right, Sarah. I completely agree with you. It helps with freedom. Freedom of choice. Freedom to be a human being," I said. "The Quran is subject to interpretation and influenced by political motives."

"And God is really for all of us," Sarah added.

"Absolutely," I said, checking the time on my phone. "It's getting so late. Thanks again, Sarah, for the documents and the delicious konafa."

"No way!" Mo said. "Where are you going that early? We were going to invite you downtown."

"I really want to stay but I need to go downstairs and get back to studying."

"Wait, study isn't everything," Mo said. "You're working hard on it and need time off."

"Sarah, let's go clean up," Rasha suggested, shuffling into the kitchen. Sarah gathered the plates on the tray and trotted behind her, lowering her head as she moved past me and smiling shyly.

"Mo, Canada is hard. The relicensing is difficult. I have all these textbooks piled on top of my kitchen chair downstairs that I need to know. Thousands of pages," I wrung my hands. "Did you ever want to go back?"

Egypt has its issues, but life was easier back home. I didn't need to figure out why my shirts shrank or became miscolored and turned pink. I destroyed so many of my fine clothes before I stopped trying to do my own laundry. The only clothes I dare try to wash are jeans, underwear, and socks. But dry cleaning is expensive and I hate asking my parents for money.

"What do you mean?" Mo asked.

"I have to do everything myself. I'm learning, like a kid. I went grocery shopping for the first time in my life when I came here. All these questions I was asked—points card, bag or no bag, donate money for charity. I didn't know what to do. Learning how to use the vacuum cleaner was a disaster—once I finally figured it out, I tried to change the bag and it broke. Garbage went everywhere. I was on my hands and knees cleaning it up."

Mo laughed. "I'd have done the same, I'm sure, if I didn't have Rasha. It's difficult. We didn't have as much house help as you did, but we had some. We had family to help. Here, we don't. Rasha finds it difficult and it's hard on her. She does so much here."

"Having a wife would help a lot," I said. "I'm so tired of microwaving falafels and eating pizza. At first it was fun, having this American experience—right out of the box in front of the TV, watching football. Now I look at the pile of boxes in the corner of my kitchen and I get so upset. I'm thankful that you invite me upstairs for dinner, but I miss my mom's food."

I recalled the big family dinners, with a spread of caucherie, macaroni with béchamel sauce, stuffed grape leaves, and konafa. Always the konafa. There was something so soothing about Mom's cooking. Eating it was like having a spoonful of love from Mom.

"Real Egyptian food melts the heart in a man," Mo said. "I'm lucky to get that every day. I know I am."

"Mo, my parents figured out so much for me," I said. "You know how it is. They influence your university program, your profession, and then start putting potential wives in front of you the day after graduation."

"Yes, my parents did something similar. They all do, don't they?" Mo asked. "They're really there for us."

My parents couldn't help me now. Everything was so new and confusing.

"Yousef, it wasn't easy for us when we came. But we're here for our kids."

"I don't have any kids," I mumbled to myself. I didn't know how I could've ever managed to have a family like Mo. It was a relief to me that I didn't have to juggle a job, recertification, a wife, and children right now.

"That's something to think about," Mo said. "Life is easier in Egypt, at least for people like us, but think about why you're here. Egypt, politically, isn't good for everybody. Don't be shy to come more often for dinner. Rasha has a good helper now."

CHAPTER 12

Two disastrous attempts at sex somehow obliged me to accept Janelle's invitation to go camping in the Canadian wilderness. In Boy Scouts, we thought spending one night in the desert was the real wilderness. Agreeing to risk my life would more than exonerate me.

Janelle picked me up for camping in the rental car at the perfect time, just like I had planned, when Mo and his family left for their daily errands. Good thing Egyptians like to do things in groups. I didn't like lying to them about some fake pharmacy training, but they'd never let me go camping. Bears. Wolves. Danger. Keep Yousef safe, just like Mom expects.

On our way to Mont Tremblant in Quebec, we travelled the verbal world together. She spoke of her heritage (Scottish, French, Swedish-American, and Indigenous), and I regaled her with stories of my Bedouin family.

After we checked-in, she quickly put up the tent herself, throwing the cots and sleeping bags inside and zipping up the tent screen.

"Done! Now we need to keep the screen closed, or we'll be eaten alive by mosquitos," she said, waving both hands in the air.

She leaned in closer.

"This Canadian variety is particularly vicious and dangerous."

I nodded, my eyes expanding.

"They particularly like Egyptians," she said, lunging and pinching me lightly with her hands all over my torso.

I jumped back, then roared, embracing her. "Now, you be nice to me this weekend. No teasing. I'm still afraid of the bears."

"They're more afraid of you, don't worry," she said.

"Do you have a gun?"

"Gun?" she laughed. "I don't own a gun. My God, nobody brings guns camping. I don't even know anybody who owns a gun. Do you think we're in the U.S.?"

"How do you protect yourself?"

"Don't wave a steak in front of a bear," she said.

"I'm serious," I said, stepping back from her.

"So am I. Don't scare them on the trail. Make lots of noise, and keep food locked up and in the car. Yousef, don't worry about the bears. I won't even play any jokes on you."

"I hope not. Or when you come to Cairo I'll play jokes about the camels."

"You would not. You're too nice. And so am I—I left my bear recordings at home this weekend, so you won't be awakened by growls," she teased. "We'll be fine. Statistically, we've got a greater chance of being hit by lightning than being attacked by a bear."

"Let's hope that we'll not have either," I said, scanning the dense wilderness. There could have been a million animals looking at me now and I'd never know. The forest was so thick. "God willing."

"Come, I'll show you what else I brought."

Janelle put on a dark green mesh jacket with a hood. "The bugs can't get through. Here, I'll help you put on your bug jacket," she said, helping me slip it on.

We faced each other through the face mesh. I felt transformed from my designer pants and Italian leather shoes into an authentic bushman. Can I say, like a "real" Canadian?

"Do I look as funny as you do?" Janelle asked.

"Probably funnier," I said. "Let's get a selfie of this."

I pulled Janelle close to me and positioned my camera. "Janelle, look," I said. "We look like a couple."

"A couple of what?" she asked, wrapping her arms around me.

"We look like we belong together."

After snapping the picture, Janelle broke free from me.

"Come on, Yousef. The jackets are for the hike. Fire time!" Janelle announced.

As Janelle built a fire, she described the steps, first making a tipi of small branches and crumpled up pieces of newspaper, lighting them, then adding bigger pieces of wood as the smaller ones caught fire. She waved the fire with her stack of newspapers, pushing the flames back and forth, at times seeming to extinguish them, before they once again caught life, coming back with more ferocity. It snapped, crackled, and hissed, occasionally sending a spark in my direction, which I jumped away from. Just like life, I mused.

"Yousef, it's tofu dog time. You're going to make them for us."

Janelle pierced two tofu dogs on a stick and thrust it into my hand. "Keep the dogs above the fire, not in it."

"We call these sausages in Egypt. Or saucisse."

"Then keep the saucisses above the fire," she said, winking, then twirling off to perform another task.

As I dangled the tofu dogs over the fire, I watched Janelle move around the campground gracefully, like it was her stage—placing a tablecloth on the table and setting out the napkins, cutlery, and plates. She took out containers of salad from her car along with mustard, ketchup, and buns.

"You thought of everything, Janelle," I said.

"I tried," she said. "It's just a natural habit for me now."

The flames mesmerized me and drew me in, in a peaceful, enchanting way. No stress of technology connectivity, traffic, or demanding customers.

We ate dinner, washed the dishes, and then sat on a campfire log, watching the flames as the sun went down. In the darkness, the fire of the other campers—yellow flames showing from behind the trees—surrounded us.

"I feel hypnotized out here," I said, taking in the sound of the fire tangled with the calls of nature.

"It's the wilderness trance, I get it," she said. "When we were kids, after the sun went down, we'd try to out-scare each other with ghost stories. Do you want to hear a ghost story?"

I wrapped my arm around Janelle and drew her close. "I'd rather hear more stories about my wonderful Janelle. What else did you do as a child? I've bored you enough with my stories of Egypt."

Janelle was silent for a moment, then said, "I guess you won't believe me if I say we built igloos and fed our sled dogs."

"Janelle, I'll believe all the words that you say. I hope you know that," I said, rubbing my hand up and down her arm. She pressed herself against me.

"Starting when I was about fourteen years old, I began going into the wilderness. It's quite honestly, where I replenish my soul."

"Did you come here with your family?" I asked.

"Only when I was really small. Most times I've been here, it's been by myself. I never get tired of it."

"Don't you get lonely?"

"Not really. Not surrounded by all this. I see the birds around me, the squirrels. Groundhogs. They keep me company. They keep me in the moment."

She met my eyes. "I love watching the animals. They're always moving, searching, finding. Maybe to build a house. Get food for their babies or fill their own bellies. They're rarely still, except if they're sleeping. It's a good philosophy, Yousef. Keep moving forward. Forget the past."

What past does Janelle need to forget? I think she has secrets to tell me.

"Do you get scared?" I asked.

"Sometimes, but you know, I try to remember the statistics. Statistically, campers aren't attacked by animals."

"You've more faith in statistics than I do," I said. Egypt was full of statistics for everything, but how much could you believe?

"Look at this big black sky full of stars. Yousef, a lot of women go to the spa. For me, I come here. This is my sacred place where I feel safe. I'm so happy to share it with you. We can keep coming back here together."

She sat on my lap and wrapped her arms around my neck. "I feel safe with you, Yousef. I love waking up to your love messages and having our video call at the end of the day. I love that. I love how you try new things about Canada and encourage me to be me. It's the only person I am."

I pulled her closer to me and kissed her forehead.

The fire had died down, nearing the end of its life. Janelle disappeared into the black night for a quick trip to the campground toilet while I doused out the last of the flames.

Suddenly I heard a loud howling. Many howls, one after the other. An entire pack of wolves circled the campsite, tracking Janelle and me waiting to pounce. God, please protect.

I ran into the car, locking the doors, only rolling down the window enough for Janelle to hear my pleas: "Janelle, come into the car right now!"

Silence. She must still be in the bathroom. Maybe I should go get her, but she has the only flashlight. I'd surely run into one of the wolves on the way. Oh, my God. Janelle, my beloved. My sweet. Where are you? I continued to call out to her every few seconds.

This camping trip was a disaster. I knew that I shouldn't have come. Why wouldn't people have guns? My God. My God. What to do?

"Yousef, Yousef!" she cried. "I could hear you yelling all the way from the bathroom. What's wrong?"

"Janelle, get in the car. The wolves have surrounded us." I unlocked the car door. "Get in now!"

"The howling?"

"Janelle, get in. Don't waste time!"

Janelle's laughter filled the air even more than the howling. She held her sides as she laughed even more. "Did you see any?"

"Why are you laughing? Janelle, don't put your life at risk."

"Yousef, come out."

"I don't think it's safe."

"They don't like how we taste."

"Janelle, I'm not joking. I heard them."

"I know you heard them," she said, opening the car door. "Everybody did. Anybody within two hours heard them. They stay in the forest. Come out of the car."

I hesitated, then stepped out and ran into the tent.

"You'll be safe in there," Janelle called out. "Wolves can't undo tent zippers."

CHAPTER 13

The following day, Janelle jumped out of the tent like she had springs attached to her feet, making us oatmeal and coffee. Today she wanted to go swimming.

After breakfast, we walked hand-in-hand down the gravel path to the empty beach. Beaches in Egypt were always so crowded.

The sun had risen high into the sky and sparkled like diamond tips on the calm water. Serene and beautiful. Small enough for me to swim across. While there were only a few lakes in Egypt, I loved swimming in the Mediterranean Sea at our summer home in Alexandria and the Red Sea across from Saudi Arabia in the winter.

Janelle dropped her day bag and laid two beach towels on the sand. She took off her t-shirt and pants, revealing a red bikini, and once again I delighted at the sight in front of me. The bikini packaged her nicely into this sexy wrapping that I wished to take off when the time was right. Hopefully soon, when I manage my nerves. She definitely wasn't shy.

Settling onto my towel, I stretched my body on the ground, admiring her body. What more could a man want? Nature and a beautiful woman. I enjoyed the dirty thoughts that invaded my mind.

"You're not changing?" she asked, pointing at my polo shirt and jeans.

I shook my head. "Right now, I'm happy just to be looking at you."

"Suit yourself," Janelle said, lying beside me on her stomach. Her behind was so round. More dirty thoughts rushed in.

"Suit myself," I repeated, half-closing my eyes and blocking the sun. That didn't seem to be the proper response. A suit. For myself. I'll have to look that one up. Up. Now I'm sounding like a Canadian.

Janelle reached behind her bikini top and unlatched the clasp. How bold. What'll I ever do with her? At least she's lying on her stomach and her breasts are hidden. I closed my eyes.

"Yousef, I want to go swimming," she said, tapping my arm.

"Sure, Janelle, in a few minutes, please."

"I'm going now," she said, sitting up and quickly removing her bikini bottoms.

"Janelle, what are you doing?" I screamed. "Are you crazy?" I grabbed my beach towel and jumped up to cover her, but she'd already begun running toward the dock.

I ran after Janelle, but she was fast. I hadn't run since high school, but I was taller than her and had a longer step. When she realized I had nearly caught up, Janelle cupped her breasts and quickened the pace.

"Try to catch me!" she squealed.

Continually scanning the beach for people slowed me down, but I needed to make sure that nobody was around to call the police.

Janelle reached the end of the wooden dock and suddenly stopped, teetering like a car on the edge of a cliff.

I stopped within a few feet from her, with the towel open wide, ready to catch her, like a dogcatcher prepared to seize the right moment of opportunity.

"Janelle, what are you doing? You've gone crazy on me!"

"Crazy, crazy, crazy," she teased. "No, not really. We have a name for this: skinny-dipping!"

She outstretched both arms as she spoke, somehow looking even more naked. My God. My God. Please forgive me.

"Every year, the first one who jumps into the lake naked wins!" she said.

"Wins what!" I said, approaching her slowly, towel outstretched. "Janelle, this is too much. What if people see you?"

"Then I guess we'll be on the Internet!" she laughed.

"Janelle, please don't do this Canadian tradition, just once, for me. Don't do it."

"Fine, I won't do it."

I wiped the sweat off my brow. When I wrapped the towel around her, Janelle wrapped her arms tightly around my torso and with a sudden jerk, lunged into the lake, forcing us both to go underwater.

Moments later, our heads bobbed in the lake, Janelle laughing. My ears and face were hot even in the cool water. My inner rage rose so fast that the water around me was sure to boil. My clenched jaw pulsed.

"I don't think I've ever seen you this angry before," she said. "Yousef, I'm sorry. I thought it'd be funny."

"How could you ever think that you running naked like a crazy person and throwing me into the water with my clothes is funny?"

"Honestly, Yousef, you really need to loosen up. Embrace the culture. That's why you came here, isn't it?"

She continued. "I'm sorry that you were all wet in your clothes. I'm sorry about that. But you need to adapt. Relax and have fun."

"My God. What would my friends say? Do all of your friends do this?"

"All of them."

"Does your family do this?"

"Last time I checked, yes. It's Canadian summer culture. No big deal. Women have been allowed top freedom since the 1990s. Look it up."

I couldn't admit to her that she might be right, as I was at a disadvantage to argue, not knowing Canadian laws. In Egypt, she would surely be arrested and go to jail.

Timidly, and still looking around for people and the police, I removed my wet clothes and sandals, placed them on the dock, and rejoined Janelle in the water. As the cool water touched my bare skin, my anger subsided, replacing the heat with this feeling of oneness with nature, no separation of life from one form to the other.

Janelle pressed her naked body against mine. Her gorgeous body made me forget why I was angry, which she probably realized. Skinny-dipping was fun, I had to admit, even a bit naughty.

Janelle touched her lips to mine.

"Are you in the mood?" she teased. "Do you want to get out of the water?" She reached down and caressed me. Oh, Janelle, you will be the end of me. My face reddened.

"Janelle," I said, moving her hand away and hugging her. "What if people see us? There's no privacy here."

"People where?" she asked, spinning her head in every direction. "Okay, forget it. It was just an idea."

She dipped herself underwater. I'd like to do all these Canadian things, but not right away. I dipped my head under and chased Janelle.

I enjoyed catching occasional glimpses of Janelle's naked body as she twisted, turned, and flipped in the water, her backside rising high enough for me to see its perfect roundedness. I reached out to touch her but she'd already evaded me, turning in another direction.

When we'd exhausted ourselves swimming, we climbed out and I put my clothes back on, which had nearly dried in the hot sun. Janelle wrapped herself in a towel, and I held her hand as we walked back.

At the campsite, we changed into dry clothes and put our bug jackets on. Janelle inspected me, looking for gaps and exposed skin. Her eyes stopped at my runners. "Aren't you wearing your hiking boots?"

"I didn't bring them." Actually, I didn't have any.

"Let's go on a small hike."

"I can do any hike that you want to," I declared even louder, my hands on my hips.

"I wouldn't recommend it. These are pretty steep hikes up the mountain."

"It's not an issue," I said, pressing my hands deeper into my hips.

"Have it your way. Let's do the Centennial trail." Janelle stuffed water bottles and nuts into a backpack and handed a hiking stick to me.

"Don't you have one?" I asked.

"It's your first time up a mountain. You should take the stick."

"Janelle, I'm the man. I don't need a stick," I said, handing it to her.

"The trail is about seven hours. Are you okay with that?"

"Absolutely," I said.

"Are you sure?" she said.

"Janelle, I don't need your advice," I said firmly. "I'm fine."

She shrugged. "Have it your way. It's one of my favorites."

After a few minutes of walking, we located the trailhead behind some thick trees and started our hike. Janelle forged ahead of me in her big construction-looking boots with thick heels, pushing branches out of the way with her hiking stick and charging forward to the next trail marker.

We didn't talk much, except when she periodically pointed at a tree and told me the name as she marched on. Spruce. Birch. Maple. Fir. Others. I became so absorbed in her rhythm, how she was like a soldier. She'd have disappeared entirely if I had stopped to examine the trees further, touch their leaves, crush them and let the new smell come into my nose. Egypt didn't have any forests, just grasses and some trees if Egyptians planted them, like palms or Cyprus. A forest was a big oxygen blanket, wrapping itself around me. Pure and nourishing.

I struggled to keep up but pretended otherwise and kept my heavy breath to myself as much as possible. Still, I think she sometimes heard me heaving.

"How are you doing back there?" she asked.

"Perfect," I said, only able to utter one word. These ups and downs were hard. A steep up. Then big down. Then up. My legs had never moved that way before. There were desert mountains in Egypt that we climbed, but a camel took us up. After the first hour, my pace slowed.

"Everything okay?" she asked.

"Fine," I said, stopping to rub aching Achilles tendon and calves, giving them impromptu massages when Janelle wasn't looking. "What a beautiful spot to look out," I said. "Do you want to stop here?"

"There's more beautiful spots ahead, on top of the mountain," she said, then added, "Do you need a break?"

"No!" I cried. "I'm fine!"

"Suit yourself," she said.

"I'm suiting myself," I whispered. "In a cheap suit that doesn't fit."

We climbed higher and past a scramble, where we used our hands to pull ourselves up.

"They created this hike to celebrate the park's 100th anniversary," she said.

Every step was painful. "Great idea. A real celebration."

"We're coming to the main part, the summit," she said.

I'd get a break here, thanks be to God. Now I eyed her stick with envy, how she casually used it to push leafy branches out of the way to clear the path for herself. I could've been using it to ease my sore knees. She could've been more insistent about giving the stick to me.

When I caught up to Janelle, she was in an open area with a spectacular view of the mountains and the winding river far below. I'd have enjoyed it just as much if a helicopter had brought us.

Canadians were hardy people. They weren't sitting around in shisha cafés smoking tobacco and drinking coffee. No Egyptian woman I knew could do this hike, and likely not most of the men.

"Really God's land," she said. "I love it every time I come here. Feel how the sun hits us, like God is embracing us."

We stood there in silence.

"I feel on top of the world. We're so high up," I said, using the opportunity to inhale more air, grabbing it with my nostrils and sending it down my legs.

"About one thousand feet," she said.

"As tall as the Eiffel tower," I lamented, "Without the elevator." No wonder I ached.

"Are you doing all right, Yousef?"

"Of course I am," I said. "Are there no animals here?"

"There are lots of animals," Janelle said. "They've probably already heard us and run away. A bear can smell us hours away."

"What do we do if we see one?"

"They can't stand the sight of two human beings kissing and hugging each other. We should do that."

Too tired to protest properly, I raised my eyebrows at her.

"Like I said," she said, "most animals already know we're here. They already left. But if one comes near, you have to stay and fight. Not run. Make lots of noise, wave your arms to make yourself look bigger to them, and fight. Now I'm being serious."

"Do you know anybody who had to fight?"

"Nobody. But there was a time when I was a little girl playing with my brother in a meadow, and we came across two baby bears. We played tag. We ran after them, and they ran after us. They were wonderful little playmates."

"What happened?"

"My grandfather yelled at us to come back to our tent. We were furious at him for wrecking our fun. But now, of course, we know he saved our lives. Things could've turned out quite differently. Are you ready to go back?"

I wanted to rest but didn't want to admit it. I knew my face gave me away when Janelle whispered, "Maybe we should take a break. I'm a bit tired."

She sat on a rock and sipped her water, eating the nuts, then I joined her. My legs would never forgive me.

The way back was somehow even more painful than the way there. Each step shot pain up my legs as we descended the mountain. I kept my curses to myself each time I heard Janelle humming or singing quietly ahead of me.

At the campsite, I sat on my log and kept my pain to myself. The log felt like a recliner to my buttocks compared to the pain in my feet and calves.

"How was the hike for you? How do you feel?" she asked.

"I could do it again tomorrow," I lied.

"What a great idea," she said. "We can do it the other way."

Janelle was the toughest woman I'd ever met. Or man. I closed my eyes and prayed she'd change her mind by morning.

CHAPTER 14

I'd never felt good about lying to Mo about Janelle, especially as he was counting his prayer beads as he regularly did, moving his finger and thumb to the next bead each time, whispering a praise to God the All Mighty. Still, at the same time, I didn't want him to report back to Mom and cause a big family upheaval. Now that we'd been together for many months, it was time to reveal her.

"Mo, I've met a friend," I said, shuffling pharmacy prescriptions, then setting them down.

"Who? Where did you meet him?"

"Her. I met her at a café."

Mo put away his prayer beads. "I thought you were going to say that she was a customer. I would've fainted. You know the rules."

"Mo, I completely understand. No worry about that. I'm studying pharmacy ethics right now. I'd never do that."

"So you met her at a café?"

"Downtown café near City Hall. We naturally started talking to each other."

"How do you naturally start talking to a stranger?"

"Just before that she almost hit me on her motorcycle, and I recognized the helmet. I was confronting her, actually."

"She rides a motorcycle? And she almost hit you? Yousef, what are you getting yourself into?" Mo gripped my arm.

Mo should learn to be less judgmental about people. It's not fair to Janelle, who he's never met.

He continued. "Yousef, what woman in Egypt rides a motorcycle? You never know what they will do. They have bad judgement."

"Mo, we're in Canada," I said confidently. "Women drive motorcycles."

"Only some of them do. Very few of them. And the ones that do, I'm not sure I'd ever want to get to know them. You know what I mean?"

"I guess I know what you mean," I said, casting my eyes into the generics.

Once again, Mo exercised his superior right as my older cousin and Mom's eyes in Canada to tell me what to do. I was a grown man, not a little boy who needed to hold Mom's hand. Besides, Janelle and I still haven't been intimate. I bolted my head up and stared into the center of his eyes.

"We went to Mont Tremblant, a camping and skiing resort in Quebec. Four hours from here. We slept outside in a tent."

"When did you do that?"

"A little while ago," I said. "I didn't have the chance to tell you until now."

"Sounds interesting," Mo said, reviewing the pile of paperwork in front of him. "What about the animals?"

"No animals, and you rarely see them, anyway," I said, proud to say something he didn't know. "They stay in the forest."

Mo shook his head. "So you had fun camping. What else? Did she show you some other Canadian things?"

"She sure did. We had dinner cooked over a campfire. Cooking food like our ancestors did, Mo. Brought back those old stories from our grandparents, cooking over the fire in the big iron pots."

"Those old stories are priceless. You know, travelling across the desert on camels. It seems so far away now from modern Cairo," Mo said.

"We also did," I said, looking around us for customers, "Skinny-dipping."

"What does that mean?"

"Swimming without clothes on."

"What?" Mo reached for his beads. "Yousef, are you crazy? You were naked in public? You can get arrested."

"That's not true. Women can expose themselves in public for many years now."

"Yousef, going completely naked in public—what are you thinking? Honestly, what's happened to you? You'd never have done this in Egypt, but this motorcycle woman, she's showing you all kinds of things."

"Mo, I'm only doing what Canadians do. You need to relax more and integrate."

He gripped his beads even tighter. "Yousef, you're like my brother. I look out for you in every way. I've your best interests in mind. Believe me."

"You also have the old ways and you haven't integrated. You only watch Arabic TV and you don't have any Canadian friends. I get a Canadian friend, and you get upset. Maybe you're jealous."

"Yousef, that's not what I'm saying." Mo did a browser search and turned the screen toward Yousef. "Come look at this."

The Canadian law site said that toplessness is legal in Ontario, but public nudity is illegal. On another website, a man going through the drive-thru getting coffee was charged with section 174 of the Criminal Code for nudity in a public place. The employees said they were uncomfortable seeing the man's genitals.

Oh, good God. Janelle and her crazy ideas. Did somebody see me? Take photos with a long-distance lens? Maybe my genitals are sitting on a police detective's desk right now, waiting to be charged.

"Yousef, you could get deported," Mo said. "This isn't a joke. Permanent residents convicted of a crime can be forced to leave Canada. Nothing would happen to her, but you could be sent back to Egypt."

Janelle could have destroyed my dream of living in Canada. How could she? That stupid little joke could have ruined my life. The fear that rose up in me was quickly replaced by anger. Such a stupid idea. She was immature, crazy, and wild.

"Believe me, Yousef, this woman sounds like trouble."

"Mo, I didn't know this. I believed her."

"I'm sorry," Mo said. "What else do you know about her?"

At that point, my concerns were pointed at me in close range. I had to admit that I knew very little about her, beyond where she worked and living somewhere north of Toronto. I'd never met her family, didn't even know for sure if she had one. Mom calls me every day but Janelle's family rarely called, if ever. Being raised in a police state made people suspicious, but this time, I had to admit to Mo I may have been deceived.

"Mo, I have you and Rasha, and you're my family, but I don't know anybody else. I was getting so lonely. When she came along, it was magic. She's beautiful and exciting. I learned Canadian customs and traditions." I hung my head. "Or so I thought."

"Come to the mosque more," Mo said. "Prayer has saved me."

"That's obvious," I said, tapping my forehead. Among devout Muslims like Mo, it was a source of pride that their head touched the carpet so much in prayer it left a dark, red mark. "I don't remember you having that before you came here."

Mo grinned. "Yeah, my raisin is the same size," he said, touching it. "Well, maybe a bit bigger when the baby comes."

Leaning forward, Mo said, "Yousef, why don't you come to the mosque and meet some new friends?"

"You know some of them are so traditional. I don't relate to them," I said. "I wanted so badly to integrate into Canada, into my new home. I've learned so much from Janelle and enjoy her spirit and energy. I love her freedom and independence."

"This is only short-lived, Yousef. When all this excitement wears away, what will you have? I feel worried for you," Mo said. "At the very least, get to know her a bit better. Go to her house and meet her family, then you'll know what she's really like."

A customer approached the drop-off counter, and Mo greeted him. "Good day. How may I help you?"

I collapsed into the stool and sat there, frozen. Broken. I always believed Janelle and never questioned anything about her, but now it seemed I needed to question everything.

I texted Janelle.

Thank you for the wonderful camping weekend. It was so nice to be with you.

The response came almost immediately.

Y, U R welcome. Great 2 C U. Fun.

I texted her again.

I want to take you to our special place.

She replied with a question mark. I texted her.

Moroccan food on Front Street.

Her response came right away.

Luv 2!

I texted.

Saturday night?

She replied.

Yes!

So many exclamation points. She was really excited. Now for the test. I texted her again.

Perfect. Will pick you Saturday 6:30. What's your address?

Her text was delayed several minutes.

Will drive myself. At work that day. Overtime.

Not surprising that she said she was working on a Saturday and again, I can't see where she lives.

See you then.

CHAPTER 15

After a long day at the pharmacy, with customers lining up nonstop and demanding their meds, I was glad to be home. As I opened the door, banging and thumping from my basement travelled up the stairs.

"Hello? Who's there?" I called down the stairs.

Maybe Rasha was checking on the furnace room.

"Who's there? Hello?"

"Welcome, Yousef!" A voice called out. "I'm in the bathroom. I'm really sorry to bother you. I thought I'd be done cleaning."

Sarah appeared at the bottom of the stairs, wearing rubber gloves and holding a toilet brush, sweat beading on her forehead. "I'm sorry to be here when you got home."

She wore one of her old galabeyas, like many women did at home for comfort, perfect for that scrubbing job.

"No bother at all," I said, coming down the stairs. "Every time I come home, I know you've been here by the clean smell in my apartment and delicious home-baked food in my fridge. Thank you so much."

She'd only been in Canada for a short time, but already I hoped Sarah never left. Her cooking was delicious, and her cleaning skills were just as good. Egyptian women knew how to create a home, luring men in. Luring me in.

"I'll be done the bathroom in a minute, and then I'll come right out, okay?" Sarah disappeared into the bathroom.

At the kitchen table, I cracked open my pharmacy textbook to the page I last left off, client interactions and communications. To my disbelief, there was an entire methodology on this topic alone, how to talk to a customer in a moral and ethical way, to not show your personal, cultural, and religious beliefs. Customers should leave feeling respected and cared for, not judged. There was a procedure for everything. It's no wonder this country worked so well, when everything was documented, tested, and updated. When you not only needed a degree to be a pharmacist, but you had to study and pass all these exams to get the designation.

Behind me, Sarah put the cleaning supplies back in the closet, then shot up the stairs like a fast arrow.

"Sarah, wait!" I called out. "Thank you for the cleaning. I'm sorry to be a bother, but I'm not very good at cleaning. Especially toilets."

"No bother at all, Yousef. I'm glad to help. I have time on my hands until Rasha is due," Sarah said, pointing to the fridge. "I made too many grape leaves again."

"I love it when you make too much food," I said, rubbing my hands together in anticipation. "Feel free to pass any excess downstairs. I can be your big empty bin to fill up."

Sarah laughed. "I'm so happy to find somebody who appreciates my cooking. You know, my sister is also a very good cook, so sometimes we get into a friendly competition. It's nice to see that I can outshine her downstairs."

"Sarah, I'm still salivating over that konafa. You had me fooled. I really thought it was from my dear Mom."

"You must be so tired from working all day at the pharmacy. I shall make you some tea," she said, taking mint out of the fridge and turning on the kettle.

"You brought me some more mint," I acknowledged. "Are you enjoying Canada? How much have you seen yet?"

Sarah leaned against the counter. "I'm here for Rasha, but definitely, I know why you enjoy Canada. It's so clean and orderly. There's no chaos here, is there?"

I nodded. "In Kingston, at least, it doesn't take two hours to get across the city like Cairo. Is that what you mean?"

"The traffic is definitely one thing," Sarah said. "The clean air. Everything is in order."

Sarah placed the tea bag and mint into a glass, then added hot water.

She said, "Even when I was grocery shopping, people lined up. Let other people pass. They don't leave their shopping cart in the middle of the aisle. Canada is orderly."

"That's one of the things that I like about it," I said. "The predictability."

"That's the word I was looking for: predictability. So you're not spending the day losing time in chaos. You can reorganize your time to do more productive things."

"That's a really interesting way to look at it, Sarah. That's a thoughtful perspective that I hadn't realized: economics in real life."

I closed my textbook and put it back on the stack.

"I studied some economics," she said, setting the tea in front of me. She retrieved some milk and sugar. "I don't know the amount of milk and sugar you take yet," she said, taking out the teabag when it reached the color I favored.

"But you definitely know the right color," I said.

"It's a woman's way."

"How is your studying going?" Sarah asked, pointing to the stack of textbooks on the chair.

"Sarah, I'm so sorry," I said, moving the stack to the floor. "How rude of me. Please sit down. Are you not having tea yourself?"

"I wasn't going to," she said. "I need to get back upstairs to cook dinner. Rasha isn't able to do much anymore and spends a lot of time lying down."

Sarah is such a good sister. Loyal. Helpful. Kind.

"Come," I motioned with my hand, "Make yourself some tea and stay a bit, unless you find me boring."

"Not at all, actually the opposite," she responded, then immediately cast her eyes away as her face reddened like the color of the tea she poured into her glass.

CHAPTER 16

I arrived early at the Moroccan restaurant and sat at the same table as our first date. I rehearsed this evening in my head a thousand times. Played out the conversation one way, then another. I'd ask questions, then when she didn't answer them honestly (predictably), I'd ask a different way where she couldn't hide from me. Nobody makes a fool out of Yousef Fahmy El Sherif. Nobody, and certainly not some deceptive woman from Canada.

Janelle waved at me from the entrance and rushed over, wrapping both arms around me, squeezing tightly. "I'm so happy to see you. I had a horrible day at work."

"You did? On a Saturday," I said. "I'm sorry to hear that. What happened?"

"Nothing really. Just work."

"No, really," I said, locking her in a hug. "Tell me what happened. I care about your day."

"I don't know, I'm trying to forget it. I'm exhausted." She struggled loose and kissed me on my cheek. "Now we're together."

"You still have a lot of energy, and you look beautiful. Like you had a spa day," I said as I pulled out Janelle's chair for her to sit down.

"Yousef, you're such a gentleman, really. I'm gushing."

Right now, I don't care what gushing means. And it's probably a lie, anyway.

"Notice this is the same table as our first date? I wanted to plan a romantic evening for us."

"So lovely. Yousef, it's so thoughtful."

After ordering food and ginger ales for both of us, I ran at the mouth about my day, that Mo was very patient in teaching me the pharmacy software even when I made mistakes. I kept hinting about my naivete and needing extra help navigating Canadian culture. She nodded encouragingly. When the food came, I knew we would be alone for a while.

"Janelle, how do you feel about me?"

Janelle put a stuffed grape leaf in her mouth. "It's wonderful to get to know you and have a lot of fun with each other."

"Do you love me?"

"I love being with you, Yousef."

"But you don't love me. I feel like I don't know you that well sometimes," I said, moving the tagine around my plate. "I wish I knew you better."

Janelle touched my hand. "Everything with time, Yousef."

"With time?" I asked. "You know everything about me. Where I work and live. My family. I don't even know where you live."

"I live in Toronto," she said. "Near Toronto," she corrected.

"Somewhere with three million other people lives my Janelle," I rolled my eyes. "That makes me feel better. What if something happened to you? How could I ever find you?"

Janelle hesitated. "Well, my house isn't as nice as yours," she said.

"That doesn't matter to me—you matter to me."

"Yousef, it matters to me—I'm ashamed of it. It's not in a nice neighborhood. It's kind of old and run-down."

"What matters is who you are and how you treat people. You could live in a tent and it wouldn't matter to me."

"Yousef, you're so wonderful. You really are," she said.

"Does your family know about me?" I asked.

"Yes," she said quickly. "How is your dinner?"

I sighed. "It'd be nice to meet your family one day."

"One day, sure. No problem. They live out of town."

"Always some reason," I said, pushing my plate away.

"You don't seem very hungry tonight," Janelle said. "Is something bothering you?"

"This entire conversation has been bothering me. I thought after knowing each other for this long that I'd know more about you."

"Yousef, this is such a wonderful evening. Why spoil it with a fight?" she said, rubbing my arm. "What's really wrong?"

I pivoted my torso squarely with hers. "Janelle, is skinny-dipping legal or not?"

Janelle laughed. "Is that what this is about?" She hit the table, exploding with laughter. "Technically, well, I don't know. But everybody does it. It's a very Canadian thing."

"Could I get arrested and deported?"

"I doubt it. I've never been arrested. Hey, where are you staying tonight?"

Typical Janelle. Not answering the questions. "I hoped it'd be with you. I'd love to sleep in the same bed as you."

"Yousef, please try to understand."

"It doesn't matter. I need to go back to Kingston, anyway. I'm working tomorrow morning."

"I feel bad that you're driving back so late."

Not bad enough, apparently, to let me sleep at your house.

I paid for the bill, then walked Janelle to her motorcycle. She unfastened her pink helmet from the side of the bike and slipped it on, turned on her bike, and waved goodbye.

I blew her a kiss, then ran to my car. Janelle exited the parking lot and turned right. I followed, careful to leave a car between us. She'd never notice me in this rental car, anyway.

Janelle said she loved being with me, but there she went, zipping around like a free woman on her little motorcycle, laughing at me. She took me for a stupid Egyptian asshole all this time. She can't know anything about love if she doesn't know anything about honesty. Maybe she has a husband and I'm just a toy on the side, as Mo inferred.

Janelle turned onto Yonge Street and went north. I followed.

I'll lay all of her lies out in front of her. One by one. Maybe she doesn't even work for a casino. Did she think I was a fool because I was new? Didn't understand English very well?

Egypt was two-thousand-year-old backward people, was that it? At least the women there behaved in ways that respected their men. Maybe Mo and my parents were right. Western women were emboldened. Too much trouble. Too free.

Egyptian women cared for their men, cooked, and did their laundry, like Rasha. They made good mothers. Janelle didn't do anything. If she was a mother, she'd put her baby on the back of her motorcycle and get on the highway.

Even Sarah made me konafa and cooked me delicious meals, leaving them in the fridge for me. Sarah was a good Egyptian woman. She was educated, respectful, and dressed the way I was used to, unlike Janelle, with her breasts and body exposed all the time with her sleeveless tops and tight yoga pants. What an idiot I'd been. Stupid.

Janelle wound her way through the streets into a place called Georgetown, then turned left and right a few more times into an established neighborhood. This neighborhood wasn't poor at all, with its large homes and luxury cars. Another lie.

Janelle signaled left and turned into a townhouse complex. I stopped and sat in the street, examining the handsome three-level brick townhomes with copper trim. Why would she be ashamed of this house? Especially when I lived in a basement. I rolled my car ahead so I could see her completely.

***

Janelle parked her motorcycle in the driveway behind a Volkswagen (of course she never told me she had a car), then pulled out her phone. My phone rang.

Immediately, I silenced the ringer. In a few seconds, I received a text from Janelle.

Hi baby. Got home. Thanks for dinner.

I texted back.

Thank you for telling me. Maybe someday I can bring you home.

It's not like that would ever happen.

She texted "Y" and then added a heart.

I unrolled my window to let some of the sweltering summer heat out. Janelle stepped inside the townhouse and yelled, "Honey, I'm home!" She closed the door behind her.

Honey. So that was it. She was married. My eyes burned and I fought hard to keep them dry. I was raging inside. My sweet Janelle turned out to be a snake. She used me and broke my heart. I must end this tonight.

I slipped out of my car and rang the bell.

A man opened the door. "May I help you?" He was a white Canadian man about the same age as Janelle, holding a beer can.

I glared at him. Her husband. My tongue was paralyzed.

"May I help you?" the man asked again. "Are you looking for the people next door? They order pizza a lot."

I couldn't say one word. How could I tell this man what his wife was doing? Would he get angry and violent with me? He would if he lived in Egypt. It's the ultimate dishonor when your wife cheats on you. A man could kill them both if he caught them in the act and probably get away with it.

I heard Janelle say, "Who's at the door, Daniel?"

"Well," Daniel said, "I'm not really sure. I thought it was pizza for next door."

"What do you mean?" she yelled, lumbering down the stairs.

Daniel sipped his beer. "I don't know if it's pizza."

"What do you mean, you don't know if it's pizza? Did you order any?"

Janelle appeared, now wearing an exercise bra and shorts, her hair in a ponytail. "Oh my god!" she said. "Yousef!"

"You know this guy?"

"Yes, he's my friend."

"Your friend," Daniel mumbled. "I'm sorry that I thought you were the pizza guy, but why didn't you just ask for Janelle?"

What the hell was going on? What was wrong with these people? Her husband didn't even seem to care that his wife was having an affair.

"Why would I just ask for Janelle?" I yelled.

"So you're not standing there gawking at me for five minutes like somebody reached in and pulled out your vocal cords," Daniel said louder. "What's wrong with you?"

"What's wrong with me? What's wrong with you!" I yelled.

This man was so casual about his wife. They're both screwed up. Good God, how did I get myself into this mess?

"Daniel, please," Janelle whispered, "Just let me talk to him. He doesn't know about us."

"Know about you!" I exploded. "No, I didn't know anything about you! You lied! You lie about everything! You even lie about skinny-dipping!"

"She didn't lie about that," Daniel assured. "She skinny-dips everywhere. She doesn't care who's watching."

"That's not what I meant! You people are crazy!"

A woman with blond hair appeared at the top of the stairs, wearing a short yellow nightgown. "What's going on?" She put her elbows on the railing setting her face on her hands, smiling at the action unfolding.

"Meghan, it's okay," Daniel said. "Just another one of Janelle's boyfriends."

Another one? So there was a long line of men in front of Janelle. I should have known. Mo was right.

"My God," I said, pointing at the second woman. "You have two wives! I'm the one who's supposed to have more than one wife, not you. Janelle, what else are you lying about? I'm finished with you."

I ran from the house into my car, taking a moment to compose myself to prevent a complete breakdown. I shouldn't drive in this condition. I knew that. But I also needed to get out of here.

Janelle ran toward me in her bare feet. "Yousef!" she screamed.

"Look at her," I said out loud. "In her bra and shorts. Looking disgraceful. Typical."

An old lady sitting with her large dog called out to Janelle. "You guys at it again?"

She said to me, "Always exciting in that house. Don't know who's living there anymore or what kind of whorehouse it's turned into."

"Whore what?" I asked.

Standing between my window and the old lady, Janelle glared at her, then returned her focus to me. "Yousef! Wait! Why did you follow me?"

I looked away.

"Come on," she said. "I was going to tell you everything. You didn't need to follow me like that."

"But you did if you wanted to know the truth," the old lady said.

"Shut up!" Janelle yelled to her.

"I'll get some popcorn," the old lady said.

"This isn't your entertainment. This is my life," Janelle snapped. She positioned herself in front of my car, then threw both hands on the hood, shouting, "I'm not leaving. You have to run me over."

I yelled, "I don't have to run over you. I'm backing out."

"You can run over her," the old lady shouted. "I won't say a thing. They're ruining the neighborhood."

Janelle ran to the back of the car and screamed, "Do it! Run me over! I deserve to die!"

"Janelle, I'm a pharmacist. I care about my reputation, so get out of here. You people are crazy."

The old lady called out, "I can attest to that. They really are crazy. They say I'm crazy, but now it's been confirmed. They're really crazy."

Janelle hissed at her. "Go inside, you old hag!"

She waved her index finger in the air at Janelle. "Your lifestyle is catching up to you. That's what's happening. Nobody has two men."

"See, Janelle? All Canadians don't have two men. It's not normal."

Janelle screamed back, "Of course it's not normal. I know that. Yousef, please talk to me."

In my rear-view mirror, I saw that Janelle had jumped on top of my bumper and flattened herself against the rear window. What a spectacle she was. This was humiliating. She better not damage the car.

Janelle yelled, "Go ahead! Drive away!"

I turned on the ignition and revved the engine. "Get off my car."

"No, Yousef. Only if you agree to talk to me."

"Get off my car."

"Talk to me!"

"Get off my car or I'll call the police."

"And tell them what? Somebody is sitting on your car? Talk to me!"

Dammit, she's right. And I definitely didn't want the police called.

"All right! I'll talk to you!"

Janelle paused, crawled across my roof, and hung her face upside down in my window. "Yousef, I'm so sorry," she whispered. "I'm so sorry that I've hurt you."

I stared straight ahead.

"Daniel was never my husband. We were living together until he cheated on me. We agreed to keep sharing the house until I had enough money to buy a condo. You've no idea how sorry I am. I never wanted you to find out about Daniel."

"Do you work at a casino? Or is that another lie?"

"Not a lie. It's true. I work at a casino. I'm a help desk analyst."

My clenched jaw throbbed under my tight skin. "Then why can't you afford your own apartment?"

"Bad boyfriend decisions," she said. "One guy took my money. My life's savings."

"How can I believe anything you say anymore?"

"Because I promise to be one hundred percent honest with you from this point forward. No matter what."

She's never said those words before. I turned off the ignition.

"Yousef, please tell me what I can do to make this up to you. How can I show you how much I care for you?"

I turned toward Janelle, who was still dangling upside down in my window. I searched her face for the openness I felt I never got from her. It was hard to do that looking at an upside-down head.

"Too much blood going to your head."

"If I faint will you save me?"

I stared straight ahead. "I'm not sure."

"Come on, Yousef. Tell me what I can do to make this better."

"You want to know how to make it up to me?"

"Yes," she begged.

"Introduce me to your family."

"Oh," Janelle fell silent. She slid off and knelt beside my car, peering into my face.

"That's complicated," she said.

"Do it," I said. "I need to know that you're serious about our relationship."

"They live out of town."

"Then our relationship is over."

"Okay, okay. Yousef, I'll do it. I'll introduce you to my family."

Finally, I'm so tired now. My brain was numbed and my whole body was aching from the stress.

Janelle interrupted the silence. "Are you happy now?"

I nodded, not able to talk. What an ordeal.

"Are you okay, Yousef?" Janelle shouted, running to the other side of the car and getting into the passenger seat.

"I'm fine, just tired. This was stressful," I said. "I still have to drive back to Kingston tonight."

Janelle side-hugged me and whispered, "No, you don't have to. It's late and you're tired. Please stay here with me tonight."

"Stay here, with you and Daniel?"

"And Meghan," Janelle reminded.

"And Meghan." I rolled my eyes. "What'll Daniel say?"

"He doesn't care. I've met all of his girlfriends. We've gotten used to it. Come on, I could really use some snuggling tonight," she said, tugging my hand. Tears welled up in her eyes. "Yousef, I don't want you to leave me tonight."

This was the first time that I felt how much she loved me. "All right, I'll stay with you."

Janelle grabbed my hand and kissed it. "Thank you, Yousef. Thank you for being so understanding."

As we drove past the old lady into Janelle's driveway, the old lady shouted at us, "Damn swingers. You're ruining the neighborhood."

"A swinger?" I asked Janelle. "What's that?"

"Never mind," she said.

CHAPTER 17

I'd been awake for hours lying beside Janelle and watching her sleep. Last night was like a horror movie. All that craziness of Janelle jumping on top of my car screaming and her neighbor watching it like she was in a movie theatre. Glad that was over. If it was the only way to see how much Janelle loved me, then my plan worked. Today I'd finally meet her family, which will bring our relationship to the next level.

It'd have been so much easier to do it the Egyptian way—all of our parents meet and agree that I'd create a future with Janelle. But I didn't want the rest of the Egyptian way—the family fighting over how much my family would pay, where we'd live, where I'd work, and so on. Even though last night was beyond crazy, it's now settled and ended spectacularly.

I'd had a lot of anxiety about being intimate with Janelle. Whether I'd do it the right way. Would she enjoy it. Somehow it came so naturally to us that I admonish myself about why I had waited so long. Our bodies flowed together. Sex was simply incredible. This complete rush of feeling in my entire body. There are no words for it.

Pepper jumped on top of the bed and licked her face. She opened her eyes and petted him.

"I could sleep for a week." She smoothed her hand over my chest. "Last night was mind-blowing. You were amazing."

I smiled. "Did you like it?" I asked.

"I loved it," she said, sitting on top of me. "Want to do it again?"

Pepper jumped off the bed. I was beginning to see the advantages of boldness. I traced my hands around her breasts and rubbed her nipples, stiffening them. "Maybe," I teased.

"I never thought you'd have so much sexuality inside of you," she said, rotating her hips on top of me.

Thinking about the night before made me want to do it again. Without saying a word, I flipped Janelle onto her back and entered her. She was already ready for me. This woman will break me.

After another round of passion, we laid on our back, holding hands. I'd never get tired of the rush of feeling overtaking my entire body.

Janelle rubbed my tummy. "Baby, do you want some coffee?"

"After that, yes, I think I need some coffee," I said, half-closing my eyes in pretend sleep.

Janelle laughed. "You're young and strong. We could do this all day long."

"I think I better have that coffee, then," I said. "Don't get mad at me if I say I'm surprised you can make coffee. How do you do it?"

"I put the pod in the machine and press the button."

I laughed, then tickled her tummy. She giggled.

"What if the machine breaks?"

"Walk across the street to the café."

"Janelle," I said, "I'm glad you don't have to take the cooking test."

"What's that?"

"Before a woman marries, she cooks for her mother-in-law to see if she's good enough to marry her son."

"You're kidding me. That's like something out of the nineteenth century."

"It's true," Yousef said. "It still exists somehow, but it's disguised as a family dinner. A welcoming of the families. Underneath all that hospitality, the mother-in-law is noting the quality of the food."

"What if I made a frozen dinner?" she asked. "It's pretty hard to screw that up."

"Janelle, what'll I ever do with you … or without you." I pulled her close and Janelle eased into my arms.

"Now that I've passed the cooking test, at least theoretically, do you want a coffee?"

"I'd love some coffee."

"I'll make it for you and bring it upstairs."

"What," I said, "Janelle, the tough motorcycle woman, is going to bring her man a coffee in bed?"

"I don't want you to get beat up by my husband," she teased.

I laughed. "I'll come down with you. I'll cook us breakfast."

"I thought you didn't know how to cook."

"I know a few things," I assured.

We dressed, then went downstairs into the kitchen. Pepper followed, wagging his tail the entire time. Janelle opened the sliding doors and let him outside.

"Oh crap," she said, looking into the fridge, "There's no eggs."

"Janelle, they're in front of you," I said, pointing to the box of eggs.

"That's not my side."

"Your side? Like a country border?"

"A bit. Wait a second," she said. "It's okay to use them. Let's say the enemy has crossed the line in the past and should expect some retribution. Let's boil them."

Janelle set four eggs in a pot, then put it on the stove. "I'm going to have a shower. You know how to boil eggs, right?"

"Of course I do. Don't worry."

She smiled. "Start adding water to the pot," she said as I patted her behind. Janelle disappeared up the stairs.

I reached for my phone and googled 'how to boil eggs.' It shouldn't be complicated, but how much water should I put in? What temperature? For how long? What if the eggs cracked—will water get in and destroy them?

As I was focused on my research, Daniel came into the kitchen. "Good morning, uh—" Daniel said, tapping his forehead.

"Yousef," I said. "You can call me Joseph if you want. That's the English version."

"Ah, yes, Yousef," Daniel said. "I never heard that name before."

"Not a problem," I said. "How are you?"

"Fine, but I can't believe I slept at all after all that drama last night. Neighbor yelling, Janelle yelling. What a racket. Janelle can be quite the tornado."

"I'm happy everything was resolved."

"Until the next tornado," Daniel said. "I'm used to it, but not everybody can take it. What a fiasco that was. Typical Janelle, though. Seems like something is always a little crazy around here."

Daniel put a pod in the coffee machine. "Meghan says I'm too nice." He shrugged. "Have you met Janelle's family?"

"Not yet."

He placed a mug in the coffee machine, and the coffee whirred and sputtered into his cup. He sighed heavily.

"Nothing I'd want. Bunch of backwater rednecks. Some of them are downright scary. I'm glad they're not part of my life anymore."

Janelle never mentioned any of this. Never talked about her family. "Everything will be fine," I assured. "I love her."

"I loved her, too, but a man can only take so much of everything. You know what I mean?" Daniel sat at the counter with his coffee, chuckling to himself.

Why would Daniel say all these bad things about Janelle? It was so strange to me. Were they true? I didn't know, but I needed to defend her. "I see," I said. "Well, I really love her."

Daniel sipped his coffee. "You'd have to." Shrugging his shoulders, he continued. "Doesn't cook or clean. Parties too much. You don't know her very well. Anyway, you believe I don't have two women now, right?"

"Yes," I said, nodding my head. "I do."

"I could barely handle one. I don't know how you guys do that over there— four wives, isn't it? I can't imagine," Daniel said, shaking his head. "What do you do with four women? They'd chase me out of my house. Try living with these two—some days I spend the day dodging bullets."

"I remember my grandfather saying," I said, "if you're going to marry more than one wife, marry four of them. They'll fight with each other and leave you alone. Maybe you need two more."

"Two more? Shit," Daniel said. "I have to deal with these two and then I have to deal with the neighbors. Some of them think we're swingers. The old guy next door keeps hinting that he wants to be part of the action. He's actually jealous of me."

"Swingers, yes, I think I heard that last night," I said, leaning against the counter, making a mental note to look that word up.

"If he knew what I had to put up with, he wouldn't be jealous. He'd pity me," Daniel said, turning towards the pot. "You're cooking eggs? I'm glad you can cook, Yousef. That's a survival skill you'll need being with Janelle."

I glanced at my phone, stuck on the boiled egg search. "I'm sure we'll find a way."

"Good morning, Janelle!" Daniel announced as Janelle came into the kitchen, his tone instantly changing the mood. He stood up and drained his unfinished cup in the sink. "I gotta go grocery shopping. My side of the fridge is looking pretty bleak these days."

"Make sure you get some eggs," Janelle said. "Once in a while, I've been known to cross enemy lines."

"Janelle, Janelle," Daniel said. "We're trying to establish a peace agreement now, right? You two have a great day. Nice talking with you, Yousef."

Daniel slid past Janelle, whispering, "I heard you last night. And this morning."

"Finally! Do you want to borrow my noise-cancelling earphones?"

Daniel rolled his eyes as he left the kitchen.

Janelle hugged me. "Things okay?"

"Janelle, everything is perfect."

"Did you get sidetracked?" she asked, pointing to the pot.

"Yes, sorry," I said, motioning to sit down. "I understand why you didn't tell me about your living arrangements. About Daniel. I think you probably made the best decision. I believe you and I trust you."

"I'm glad you believe me," she said. "I was worried that you would kick me out of your life. I'm sorry I hid this, but I wasn't lying when I said I was embarrassed about my home. It was just for a different reason. Living with Daniel and Meghan is embarrassing."

"I understand," I said, kissing her hand.

"Why don't I make us breakfast," Janelle suggested.

"I said that I would," I said.

"And you got so far, in that search for how to boil an egg," she said, pointing at my screen.

"This time, I'll let you boil the eggs," I said, straightening my back.

"Have a seat in the great room. Make yourself comfortable," Janelle said. "I'll only be a few minutes. Remember, I'd fail the cooking test."

The great room had a fireplace, a large black leather sofa, and a matching chair. Sitting on the sofa, I scanned the pictures on the wall behind me. Some pictures were of Daniel and an older woman he looked like. Maybe his mother. There were also other pictures with Daniel and, presumably, other family members wearing Christmas sweaters or being in nature. Most pictures were of Daniel and Meghan doing activities, from winter skiing to summer kayaking.

The smell of the coffee and toast had snuck into the great room.

Janelle wasn't anywhere on the wall. Symbolically, at least, it was as if she was cornered entirely into the small territory of her room. Even in her room, though, there were no pictures of her family. In Egyptian families, entire walls are filled with photos of every stage of life. You can see a family's history unfold by looking at their walls.

"Yousef," Janelle called, "Breakfast is ready. We can sit at the island if that's all right."

The boiled eggs, rye toast, and coffee weren't an Egyptian breakfast like Mom's, but it was a fine Janelle breakfast.

"After breakfast, we've one last thing to do," she said. "I'd love to introduce you to my family today."

I kissed her cheek. "It'd be an honor to meet your family."

***

After travelling for two hours, we arrived at Janelle's parents' townhouse. I held the torn screen door open for Janelle while she knocked on her parents' front door, which was white once but was now battered with scuff marks and peeled paint. The flower bushes that lined the townhouse wall hadn't been tended to, and the parched, withered flowers had succumbed to the weeds around them in the July heat.

"I texted my mother," Janelle said, banging on the door. "She knows that we're coming."

Janelle slowly opened the door. "Hi, Mom!"

A man's voice bellowed from nowhere. "Your mother isn't home. She went to bingo."

Janelle gently pulled me inside. We maneuvered our feet through the pile of shoes at the door, kicking some shoes to the side to find a clean space to stand.

Janelle called up the stairs. "Hi, Dad. How are you?"

"How do you think I am? I'm old and crippled. What can an old man do?"

Janelle motioned to follow her up the stairs, over the cracked linoleum, and past the dust balls.

Janelle's father sat in his recliner, staring at the television in front of him that wasn't turned on. His white hair sat on top of his head like an unmowed lawn, seemingly covering the patches that had worn away. His yellow dress shirt, which may have been white once, was covered with stains. He had mustard on the edges of his mouth. He rocked back and forth, back and forth, surrounded by garbage bags full of faded newspapers. A full bottle of beer sat on the side table beside the chair, along with two other empty ones. He twisted his head towards us.

"Who's that?"

"Dad, this is Yousef."

"You got a new one?"

Was that a joke? It wouldn't be a joke in Egypt. It's never polite to talk about one's personal matters.

"Dad, please."

I extended my hand to Janelle's father, gently reaching downward so her father didn't have to move. His blue eyes peeking through his hair stared me down.

He grabbed my hand, seemingly attempting to jerk my arm out of my socket, forcing me to adjust my feet to stabilize myself.

"His name is Yu-stuff? What kinda name is Yu-stuff? Are you sure it's not "your stuff"? Watch out, he might be after your stuff!" he laughed so hard he began coughing and wheezing.

"You-SUFF. His name is Yousef. It's Egyptian."

"Egyptian? Do you live in a Pyramid?" Janelle's father held his gut as he laughed at his own joke. "You know, they always say us Canadians live in igloos. Can you imagine such a thing? Igloos. Nobody lives in igloos anymore. Not even the people who are supposed to, but I guess you don't know what an igloo is."

Janelle gripped my hand tightly while her father scanned my entire body. "Why do you suppose I know what a Pyramid is, but you don't know what an igloo is?"

"I don't know, sir. I'm so pleased to meet you."

"Those are the original Canadians," Janelle's father proclaimed. "Everybody else is a fake, except the British. We've been here since the fifteenth century and built this country."

"There's lots of other people who built this country," Janelle said. "The Vikings, the French, lots of other people."

"Not Egyptians," Janelle's father said, gripping the arms of the recliner and pushing himself up. He limped to another doorway leading downstairs and roared, "Hey Tommy, come up here."

"My younger brother," Janelle said, steadying her hand on my arm.

"I know who he is," her father retorted. "I'm old, not stupid."

When Tommy entered the living room, I knew immediately that he was his father's son. He had the same vivid blue eyes as his father and was also as tall as him, wearing blue jeans and a white T-shirt.

"Yeah, Dad?"

"This is Janelle's new boyfriend. You-something."

"Yousef," Janelle said.

"It's Joseph in English," I added.

"No, it isn't. That's ridiculous," her father said. "Joseph is Joseph in English, not Yousef."

I extended my hand. Tommy looked at it, then turned to his father and said, "How long do you think this one will be around?"

"Good question!" Janelle's father shot his closed fist straight into the air, like he was at a sports game. "A bet! I'm going to bet two months max!"

"That's not fair," Tommy said, "You can't pick two months. That's how long the last one was around."

Tommy got himself a can of ginger ale from the kitchen.

"Yousef, they don't know what they're talking about," Janelle whispered. "Come on, you guys. Just be nice. Yousef and I are together now."

Janelle's dad threw his arms into the air and turned to me. "She's wild, you know? Crazy, really. You sure you can handle her?"

I put my hands on Janelle's shoulders to support her, but maybe more so to keep myself upright. "It'll be fine," I whispered. I don't know why I was whispering like I was afraid, but maybe I was. My family would never have treated a guest so badly, not offering tea or sweets, and hurling one insult after another at a man standing in their house.

Her father shuffled over to a picture on the wall. "Take a look at this picture, Yustuff."

Janelle pulled me toward him. A little girl in a red-striped dress sat on a tricycle. "This is Janelle when she was four years old. She was already pretending this tricycle was a motorcycle. Vroom! She'd say. Vroom!" Her father shook his head. "I don't know where the hell she got the idea from. The rest of her family is much more sensible, but she's racing around on a motorcycle like Evil Knievel. Do you know who that is?"

"No, I'm sorry, sir, I don't."

"Well don't be sorry that you don't know anything. You're not from here. That explains everything. Sit down, sit down. Why do you keep standing?"

Janelle pushed some yellowed newspapers aside, and we sat on the sofa. "Anyway, all I'm saying is I don't know what the hell you're going to do with her. Was with a nice young man and then almost right away, we heard they split up. Ridiculous. And then I heard several others came along—several. You know what I'm saying?" Janelle's father didn't wait for an answer. "Then you come along. You think it's going to work with her?"

He continued, "Are you trying to get a green card? Is that it?"

"Dad, Yousef doesn't need a green card. He came here on his own. He's a pharmacist."

"So you're the druggist himself. Well, that doesn't surprise me. All those people over there doing crazy things, blowing themselves up. Doesn't surprise me at all that you're into drugs."

"Sir, all I know is that your daughter is very special to me. I thank God for her."

"Oh, God, yeah, you've a different God, don't you?" he said, tugging my arm, peering into my eyes. "We go to church in this country."

"Hardly anybody goes to church anymore," Janelle said, then whispered to me, "Ignore him."

"I'm not deaf or stupid. You show respect in this house," he said, waving his hand in front of himself. "Janelle, you and your yoga stuff has warped your mind. All that chanting," her father said. He turned to Tommy and asked, "What kind of God do Egyptians have?"

Tommy put his hand to his chin and paused. "Lots of different kinds. God of baboons. God of snakes. God of cats. God of frogs."

"God of frogs? I feel bad every time those buggers get stuck under the wheels of my car. Feel so bad. So maybe having a god of frogs isn't such a bad idea."

Janelle reached over and tapped her father on his leg. "Stop it, both of you. Those are Ancient Egyptian gods from thousands of years ago. They believe in the same God we do."

"They do?" her father and brother said together.

"Then you better pray to God that Janelle doesn't get tired of you in two months, or I win my bet."

Janelle's father and brother high-fived each other. Janelle's dad laughed so hard he sputtered, stopping to catch his breath.

I hoped I continued to appear stoic, and my face was clean of emotion and discomfort, though tears swelled up in Janelle's eyes. This was a disaster.

My phone rang, and I immediately silenced the ringer. It continued to buzz. Mom. "Excuse me," I said, then answered the call in Arabic. "Mom, I'm with a customer right now. I'll call you soon."

"Now he's going to blow us all up!" Tommy said, throwing his hands up into the air. "Ka-boom!"

"Get to the bomb shelter!" her father yelled. "Before he pulls the string!"

"Stop it! Both of you! You're humiliating me," Janelle yelled.

My phone rang again. Mom again. I continued to let it ring, and said, "I'm so sorry, sirs, but I have a teleconference. It was a pleasure to meet you. I look forward to seeing you again."

I extended my hand between Janelle's father and brother, hoping that one of them would grab it, but I put my hand down to relieve my embarrassment when it was left hanging in the air.

Her father and brother smirked at each other.

Once outside, I put my arm around Janelle and embraced her.

"I'm sorry," she said. "Now you know why I didn't want to bring you."

"I'm the one who should be sorry. I'll never ask you to do this again."

We walked back to the car in silence. I glanced back at the house, trying to make sense of the craziness. It was so different from the grand Egyptian hospitality I knew. Guests were served tea on a silver platter and special sweets from the bakery. We took pride in how we treated a guest, even if we didn't like them. Now I knew what Daniel meant by the chaos in Janelle's family. If Janelle and I married, this would be my future, too. My phone ringing broke the silence.

"*Salam*," I said. "How are you, Mo?"

"Good news! Rasha had her baby," Mo said. "A baby boy. We were awake the entire night."

"Thanks God. Congratulations!" I said. "How is she doing? How is the baby?"

"She and the baby are fine," Mo assured. "His name is Tahir."

"A beautiful name—purity."

"Listen, the Seboa is being prepared. You're family. You don't need an invitation."

"Of course I wouldn't miss it. Can I bring a friend?"

Mo paused. "That friend?"

"Yes, Mo, that friend."

After a few moments, Mo broke the silence in a quiet voice. "Okay, I'm sure it'll be something she's never experienced."

"Thank you, Mo. This means a lot to me."

I clasped Janelle's hand. "Let's forget today. I have some good news. My cousin had a boy. We're going to celebrate with them at the Seboa."

"What's a Seboa?"

"When the baby is born, after seven days, we have a celebration. Seboa means the seventh day."

"Like a baby shower, then," Janelle said.

"Shower? Don't think so. No, not a shower," I said. "It's a party. Egyptians never turn down a chance to have a party."

CHAPTER 18

I texted Yousef that I was at his door. I was nervous about meeting Yousef's cousins at the baby shower. What if they didn't like me? What if I screwed up some Egyptian custom?

My reading about the Seboa ceremony did nothing to make me feel less nervous. Egyptians were superstitious, warding away evil spirits by banging drums and yelling on the seventh day after the baby's birth. Seven, a lucky number, and when the baby could hear and absorb religious prayers.

The Seboa seemed so different from my friends' baby showers, where women sat in a circle and admired the almost-new mom's growing baby bump, sharing the joy their little ones brought into their lives, playing lighthearted games, and eating treats.

It's my turn to step up, given everything he's done for me, and accepting me for my little lies about living with Daniel and Meghan. For a guy who just "got off the boat" in Canada less than a year ago, he's been very accommodating and open-minded.

I've never been treated with such kindness, such respect. Most of the time, the guys jump into bed with me after a night out, and then they don't call again. It was so disappointing and it made me feel really terrible about myself. They got what they wanted, then left. Well, sometimes it was the other way around, and I got what I wanted, then left.

With Yousef, it was so different. We waited so long to be intimate, and then it was so special when it happened. The little love texts he sends me every night before I go to bed, and then the ones in the morning. Every night and every morning. It made me feel so loved. This man definitely has my heart. What a vulnerable yet lovingly tender place to be.

"Janelle, so nice you're here," he said, hugging me.

His hugs were always so welcoming. Love going right into my bones.

"Let me help you with your bag."

Inside his apartment, I changed and freshened up. "Hey, Yousef," I said, pointing to my blouse, "Did you notice my shirt that covers my shoulders?" I twirled around, shaking my booty. "And what about these baggy jeans?"

Yousef hugged me again. "I did. Thank you, that means a lot to me."

"Yousef, introducing me to your friends and family is serious. I hope they like me."

"It shows that we're committed to each other," he said. "They'll love you as much as I do."

Yousef tugged on my hand to join him on the sofa. "Janelle, there's something I need to tell you. Remember that you didn't tell me about Daniel and Meghan? You were afraid of what I'd think?"

I nodded.

"I also have a secret," he said. "I hope you won't be so upset with me."

"What is it?"

He hesitated, then said, "Mo and Rasha live upstairs."

"Your cousins live upstairs?" I flipped my hands into the air, laughing. I thought he was hiding another wife.

"So what?" I shrieked, laughing. "Why would you hide that?"

"Janelle, I'm thirty-three years old and living in my family's basement," he said.

"Can't be any worse than being twenty-eight years old and living with your ex-boyfriend and his girlfriend," I said, patting his arm. "Don't worry about it."

"Thanks God, I was so worried about what you'd think of me."

"You'd have to try a lot harder to get rid of me, Yousef," I said.

I really couldn't fault Yousef for a lie when I'd told much bigger ones. Yousef was a good man. Even being ashamed about living in his cousin's basement was a good sign because it meant that he cared about being independent and moving forward with his life and establishing himself.

"Are you ready to go upstairs?" he asked.

"Nervous," I said.

"It'll be a great night. Let's go," he said.

We went to the front of the house and Yousef rang the bell. He squeezed my hand.

"Ahlan!" Mo extended his hand to Yousef, and they embraced, kissing each other on the cheek. Yousef placed an envelope into Mo's hand, and they exchanged a few words in Arabic.

"Mo, this is my friend, Janelle," Yousef said.

Mo extended his hand to me. "Welcome. Nice you could come for the Seboa. Rasha and the baby are in the living room."

Two boys and a girl came running toward us, then stopped, hiding behind Mo.

"This is my friend, Janelle," Yousef said to them. They ran away, chasing each other down the hall. "Kids," he said, shrugging his shoulders.

I flipped off my sandals, which landed upside down. Yousef quickly flipped them back over. "It's bad luck," he whispered. Clutching his hand, I followed him down the hall.

In the living room, blue balloons had floated up to the ceiling. Set on a beautiful oriental rug were two sofas, end tables with ornate gold lamps, and a long wooden coffee table with clawed-foot legs. Sitting on the sofa was a woman who looked to be in her thirties, wearing a dark blue hijab and a loose-fitting blue dress that reached the floor. Her face was plain but pleasant, with round eyes and olive skin. Her arms were folded, holding a little white blanket, a small head with dark hair popping out. I came toward her.

"Hi, Rasha? I'm Janelle. Congratulations!" I said, extending my hand.

She accepted my hand briefly, nodding, before wrapping it around her baby again. "Thank you."

Another woman entered from the back of the room. She was younger than me and wore a fitted traditional dress to the floor that showed her petite frame. Her brown eyes were striking and exotic and lined with thick eyeliner.

"My sister Sarah, from Cairo," Rasha said. Sarah spoke to Rasha in Arabic, who nodded. They exchanged words with Yousef, then Sarah left the room.

"She's getting tea for us," Yousef said.

A few minutes later, Sarah returned carrying a silver tray with a copper tea urn and glass cups. She poured the tea into glass cups, placed a mint leaf in each, and handed them out. I sat on one of the sofas with Yousef.

Rasha's baby's moved, stretched, yawned, and wriggled within the confines of his blanket, his black hair contrasting strongly against the white blanket. His Mom looked down at him lovingly and smiled.

"A new little life. I'm so happy for you both," I said. "What's his name?"

"His name is Tahir," Rasha said. "Tahir means pure and clean, free from sin." She looked at the entire length of me, then said, "In Egypt, dignity is important."

Seemed deliberate. What more could I do than cover my shoulders and wear jeans that were almost falling off my ass.

Within a few minutes, many other friends arrived, about a dozen couples, each having two or three kids in tow. The children packed together and then disappeared to play games. About half of the women wore hijabs.

I smiled as often as possible, sitting by Yousef's side as, one by one, men shook his hand and spoke to him in Arabic, acknowledging me in English and then disappearing into Arabic conversations. At first, Yousef was holding my hand, but as he became more involved in the discussion, he used both of his hands to make his point with expansive gestures, laughing loudly and fully at times; other times, seeming to argue with his friends.

"Men talk about politics, soccer, and religion," he leaned over to me. "Women talk about children, families, and cooking."

I nodded, thinking how dreary an Egyptian woman's life must be. No fun camping, exploring, or adventures on motorcycles, but stuck inside a sweltering kitchen cooking for a family.

The women took turns holding Rasha's baby, rocking him back and forth in their arms, and cooing at the slightest expression he'd make. The baby made his rounds among the women, but the women didn't come near me. Like I was toxic.

The room had become excruciatingly loud, each person seeming louder than the person before, all at the same time. Yousef had become enmeshed in a deep, impassioned debate with Mo. He'd forgotten I was even here, glancing at me only in a perfunctory way as he collected his next thoughts for the next leg of his debate.

When I attempted to grab Yousef's hand to gain some strength to counter my discomfort, he gently pulled it away, using it along with his other hand to emphasize his point, his arms waving in the air to Mo. I forced a smile to keep myself from falling apart and crying in front of strangers. I wanted to leave and go on a long ride away from these people until he finished.

Sarah spoke to Yousef in Arabic, then went into the kitchen.

"What did she say?" I asked Yousef.

"She asked if I wanted some dessert. Some konafa."

"What's that?"

"Konafa is a dessert made from pastry and cream. And lots of sugar."

"It sounds interesting," I said, trying to throw any amount of English into the air.

"One of my favorites. My mother makes the best konafa—Sarah makes konafa like my mother."

"Maybe I could learn how to make it," I offered.

"Maybe," Yousef said. "But it's quite difficult."

Sarah returned from the kitchen with one piece of konafa on a plate, handing it to Yousef, then smiled, speaking in Arabic. "She asked if I loved her konafa. This is true," he said, gulping it down.

"Janelle, have some," Yousef offered. "I'm sure you'll like it."

I cut off a small piece and popped it into my mouth. It was very sweet and had a crunchy crust with sweet custard in the middle. "It's very good. I like it. It doesn't seem difficult to make."

Sarah brought another piece for Yousef, this one bigger than the first, then sat in the wooden chair that Yousef got for her. He quickly got absorbed in Sarah, taking in her conversation, as if taking in every bite of the konafa was also taking in Sarah, with her exotic man-trap eyes.

"Yousef," I interjected.

"One second, please," he said, "Sarah was telling me a funny story."

Sarah slipped out a smile in my direction.

As Sarah spoke, Yousef was captivated, consuming every part of her. When I tapped his leg, he gently clasped my hand, then put it back on my knee. Sarah obviously didn't speak English, but she didn't seem to mind that I couldn't understand anything. In fact, she probably liked it, so she could flirt with Yousef in front of me and get away with it. Yousef appeared so enthralled with Sarah that he didn't even look at me anymore. Finally, Sarah left.

Yousef turned to me. "Sarah is so kind. She cooks me food, which is nice when I come home from the pharmacy."

So there's flirting and food. What other f-word would fit here? There's no doubt about it. Sarah was trying to squeeze herself in and get my man. Yousef was oblivious to the tricks that women played, as most men were. Sarah wasn't getting away with this.

Yousef said, "They're getting ready for the celebrations. You'll love this."

Suddenly, all the women moved to another room with the children. Yousef winked at me and patted my back. "Go," he said. "Have fun."

I stayed sitting, not wanting to be alone with a bunch of chatter bugs who didn't speak English, but as the women and children emptied out of the room and the remaining men continued to look at me, Yousef nudged me forward. "Go," he murmured.

I trailed behind the group into the next room. A loud cowbell sound rang into the air as a woman banged a steel mortar and pestle. Immediately, the clapping and shouts of the women reminded me of the Native American warrior cries in the old western movies, and I pressed both of my hands to my ears. Somebody banged a drum somewhere among the cacophony, which felt like a physical assault thumping through my body. Not wanting to embarrass Yousef for acting like the strange Canadian, I slowly lowered my hands and endured the ear-splitting mélange of screaming, banging, and music.

Four men carried a large wooden platter into the room, the size of the surface of a kitchen table, overflowing with gifts and candy, which spilled over the sides. The children ran around the platter, stretching their arms out, trying to catch the falling pieces. They screamed and laughed each time a candy fell into their hands.

Four women held a large mesh circle, looking like one I'd seen to sort grains by hand, as Rasha placed her baby in the center. The women sang as they gently rocked the baby back and forth. I guessed this was the part of the ceremony where they cast out evil spirits and asked for God's protection over Rasha's baby.

A procession started to belly dancer music, and the children slowly danced around the room, each carrying a white candle. The children continued into the next room, clapped in by the men already there. Yousef saw me and briefly interrupted his clapping to wave at me. I cast my eyes away from him, turning my attention to the end of the procession where Rasha appeared with her baby, greeted with rowdy applause and cheer.

My loneliness was momentarily suspended by all the joy I felt in the room for Rasha and her baby. It was beautiful to have so many people celebrating her new little baby with her. And this new mother, like all new mothers, looked so beautiful.

The children continued to sing, moving around the room in a circle. A little girl, almost too young to walk, showed off her belly dancing moves. I smiled. Even the youngest girls got the beat and could move their hips like belly dancers. The men then joined the procession, and everybody paced in a circle around the room, dancing and singing. I sat at the side, caught in the hypnotic spell of the Arabic beat.

When the song ended, everybody in the room broke into loud applause and warrior cries for the proud parents, who stood together at the front of the room. Yousef, across the room, wasn't looking in my direction, continuing to talk and laugh with the men around him.

I followed the crowd to the dining room and spotted the buffet overflowing with food.

"Janelle," Yousef called out, "Come over and enjoy the feast."

He waited for me to find my way to the feast table. "The food is the best part of the evening."

I said nothing as I moved closer to Yousef.

"Egyptians love celebrations, but mostly love the food," he bragged. "Nobody is on a diet here. Grab a plate, my dear, and join in."

"There's macaroni over here," Yousef said, pointing to the steaming dish. "It's excellent—you need to try it."

I spotted the hunks of meat in the macaroni. "Does it have meat in it?"

"Yes, I'm sorry," Yousef said. "I got so excited about all the food. We'll find some vegan food. Here, give me your plate."

I handed my empty plate to Yousef, who began perusing the entire length of the feast table, putting food onto our plates. I sat on a chaise against the wall, away from the others.

The guests were entangled in conversation; a steady hum of Arabic filled the air. The children were seated at a table together, laughing and talking. Rasha and her baby were together with Mo. Yousef encircled the table, slowly examining each dish, speaking in Arabic to Sarah. Sarah laughed at his jokes—too much, and every time I heard Sarah giggle like a high-school girl, I winced.

Yousef presented a plate to me loaded with pickles, bread, beans, and salad. "I'm so sorry. I told them you were vegan, but with all the excitement, they forgot."

I examined his brimming plate of food and then my own meager portion. "I wasn't that hungry, anyway."

But I was starving. I had to satiate my growling stomach with a fucking pickle. I bit into it, then glanced up and saw Sarah smiling. It wasn't a friendly smile, but more like a cat's before it bit off a mouse's head.

"Janelle," Yousef whispered, "Eat with your right hand."

"Why? I always eat with my left hand."

"Not in front of my friends and family, please," he asked. "It's unclean."

"One hand is as clean as the other, Yousef," I said, switching the pickle to the right hand.

"Would you like some more bread? I'll get it for you," Yousef offered.

I shook my head. I was already bloated.

Again, Sarah initiated another animated conversation with Yousef. I sat beside them, eating the last of my beans. I ate one bean at a time, scrutinizing each for its shape, color, and texture, trying to stretch out time until all this was over, like it was some meditation exercise. Would I ever love some chocolate to stuff down my emotions—a big box of dark chocolate from an expensive chocolate store. I began internally drooling at the thought.

The more giggling Sarah did, the worse I felt, like she was turning the knife inside me. It sounded forced.

"Yousef, it's getting late," I whispered, tugging his arm.

"Just a moment. We're almost done, okay?"

I held back my tears. I felt so alone. Throughout the evening, the food disappeared, the noise dwindled, and the people trickled out. Rasha had already put the baby to sleep along with their other children. When nearly everybody had left, Yousef spoke to Mo and Rasha in Arabic, shaking Mo's hand.

"Thank you," I said softly to both of them. "I wish I knew how to say that in Arabic."

"No need, my dear," Yousef said. "I'm here."

You're here now, jerk. Where were you all night?

Sarah joined the conversation, replacing Rasha and Mo as they attended to other guests who were leaving. I slipped on my flip-flops and sat outside on the front steps.

What the hell was I doing here? I didn't fit in, nor could I speak Arabic. People didn't want to talk to me. Maybe they couldn't speak English very well, but no, that's not true. How could they have jobs in Canada if they couldn't speak English? This night was one big mistake. I was stupid to think I could fit in with Yousef's friends and family. So foolish to think I'd be welcomed into their home.

"Here you are, Janelle," Yousef said, sitting beside me. "I thought you went to the bathroom."

"To empty out what, exactly?" I retorted. "All the food I ate?"

"Janelle, I'm sorry about the food. I really told them. They forgot. How did you enjoy the rest of the evening?"

"How do you think I enjoyed myself? I didn't understand a word of any conversation. I ate more pickles tonight than I have in my entire life. And I'm still hungry. Fucking pickles. I'll never eat another one."

"Janelle, I'm so sorry. Why don't we get something to eat now?"

"At midnight? What do you think is open right now? A convenience store with day-old plastic sandwiches? Do you know what I call those? Funeral sandwiches. Do you know why?"

"Tell me."

"They serve them at funerals, which is what it felt like tonight."

"We can find something, I'm sure. A roti or a burrito. Even some fries."

"Never mind," I said, leading the way to Yousef's apartment door. "Who's Sarah?"

"She's Rasha's sister, I told you."

"How well do you know her?"

"I don't, really. I met her again after many years when she brought my papers from Egypt for Mom. I told you that."

"So, you don't know her and she's cooking for you?"

"I've seen her a few times," Yousef admitted.

"And she's cooking for you? Isn't cooking for a man significant in Egyptian culture?"

"All women cook in Egypt. Sisters. Cousins. Everybody."

"She seems quite enamored with you."

"What?" Yousef asked.

"She was almost fucking you on the dining room table."

"Janelle!" Yousef shouted. "Sarah is Rasha's sister." He placed his hand firmly on top of mine. "Nothing else."

He opened his apartment door, and I followed him in. "Women know women," I said. "Does she cook well?"

"It doesn't matter how she cooks. She's my cousin's sister."

"She makes konafa better than your mother."

"I try to be complimentary. It's the custom," he defended. "Janelle, please stop it. I'm not discussing this anymore. Why are you destroying a nice evening?"

"Who says it's a nice evening? For you, maybe," I said, grabbing a blanket from his bed. "For me, I almost cried the whole time. How fun do you think it was for me? Good night, Yousef."

I removed my clothes in the bedroom, then wrapped myself in the blanket and laid on the sofa.

"Janelle, come to the bed," Yousef pleaded.

"No!" I yelled out. "Ask Sarah. Maybe she'll bring her konafa and you can stuff yourselves."

"Janelle, come on. You can't sleep out here."

"I'm fine. I need a pillow. Can you bring me one?"

Yousef placed a pillow under my head. "Here's your pillow. Let me sleep out here. You can have the bed."

"Yousef, good night." I turned over, away from him, and closed my eyes. "I need to sleep."

***

The morning came too soon, with Yousef hovering around me. "Janelle," Yousef said, "how did you sleep?"

114

"Sore," I said, in a sleepy voice. Sleeping all night on this sofa gave me a backache. Then I remembered why I was out here and got mad all over again.

Yousef ran his hand down my back. I'd always enjoyed the touch of his large, masculine hands that were also warm and nurturing. He always kept his hands and nails clean and trim, like the rest of him. Rather than press into him like I usually did, I laid like a stone.

"I'm still mad. Last night was a disaster."

"It didn't go as I planned. I agree with you. I was so excited to introduce you to my friends and my family. I didn't know you'd feel uncomfortable."

I shot my head around and glared at him. "What do you mean, you didn't know? How do you think I'd feel around a bunch of Arabs all night? They completely ignored me."

I continued, "You didn't even talk to me. It was like you became one of them and just forgot about me. Why even invite me if you won't talk to me?"

"I'm really sorry. I only wanted you to be a bigger part of my life."

"I'm still pissed off."

Yousef rubbed the entire length of my back from top to bottom, and over my derrière. His hands were gentle and warm, but firm. I still resisted.

"What can I do to make it up to you?"

I knew that voice—the sincere and authentic one he usually had. And I was hungry.

I turned my body around to face him. "I still taste pickles," I said, showing him my tongue. "I'm famished. Would you make me breakfast?"

"Janelle, I don't even have eggs. You know I don't cook here. Why don't I get you some breakfast? There's a bakery close by that makes breakfast sandwiches and excellent coffee."

I could almost smell those breakfast sandwiches now. "Do they have tomatoes and lettuce? Is it organic coffee?"

"Yes, tomatoes and lettuce, and organic coffee. If it's not organic, I'll go somewhere else. My Janelle will only have organic coffee."

The thought of getting intoxicated on a steaming cup of coffee had a mitigating effect on my irritation. "That would be really nice. Yum yum. Thank you."

"I'll be back soon," he said, kissing my forehead. "I miss you already."

I watched Yousef climb the stairs. The truth was, I missed him, too. I couldn't help but fall into the warmth of Yousef. He was kind, generous, and a gentleman. He provided me that nice balance of a strong versus emotional man. Egyptians were very social, and even though the baby shower didn't go very well, I admitted that I loved the community nature of Yousef's people. Egyptians really knew how to party and how to celebrate life.

After breakfast, I'd soften toward him. I needed to learn to get over my hurt feelings. Yousef didn't have anything to do with what went wrong last night; it was the first time he'd had a Canadian girlfriend. Maybe he was adjusting at the same time I was.

Footsteps coming down the stairs behind me disrupted my thoughts.

"Yousef," I heard a woman's voice say.

Sarah! I'd recognize that bitch's voice anywhere. What was she doing, coming down at breakfast time? Naked, I sat frozen on the sofa. Maybe if I was really quiet, Sarah wouldn't know I was there.

"Yousef," Sarah said, her voice getting closer. It sounded laced with honey, just like last night.

Completely submerging myself under the blanket and laying like a corpse, I hoped she wouldn't see there was a human form on the sofa. Maybe the silence would be enough to deter her from coming closer.

"Yousef," Sarah said, her sweet voice becoming saccharin. Now she sounded like she was standing right over me. "Yousef," she said.

She stood over me, talking in Arabic. I smelled food. So that's why she was here. To have breakfast with Yousef. She probably did this all the time.

Sarah wasn't giving up or going away.

I slowly uncovered my head and face, seeing Sarah in front of me, holding a tray full of food. Sarah's happy eyes and smiling face changed instantly into shock and horror. She screamed.

Sarah dropped the tray. The plates and bowls smashed onto the floor, splattering in every direction. Steaming fried egg hit my face. Sauce landed in my hair. Dammit.

I wiped the egg away with a corner of the blanket, and my boob slipped out. Sarah screamed again and began yelling in Arabic. She scooped the food onto the tray on her hands and knees, alternating between crying and yelling at me.

I was stuck naked underneath this blanket. I couldn't move or I'd traumatize her. "Dammit," I said to myself. "My clothes are in the bedroom."

"Then get them," she yelled at me, still reassembling her food tray.

"What did you say?" I asked.

Sarah said nothing, not looking at me.

"You spoke English," I said.

Sarah paused, then in a calm tone, said, "Of course I speak English. You think us desert people don't speak English?"

"You didn't speak English last night," I shrieked, recalling all her giggling and private conversations in Arabic with Yousef. What a shit she was!

Sarah's eyes narrowed into slits like a cat eyeing the family bird. "There was no need," she said, pointing to my naked shoulders. "You have no modesty."

"Modesty! Whatever that means. I'm a free woman. There's no shame in nakedness," I said, flashing Sarah.

Sarah screamed again, then nattered nonstop to me in Arabic. She was probably sending me to hell.

More footsteps clamored down the stairs. Before me, Mo and Rasha stood, their mouths open and eyes big. Deer caught in the headlights looked more relaxed than they did. Rasha yelled, "What are you doing here? Oh my God! My children! They've been exposed to your immorality!"

She turned to Mo and yelled at him in Arabic. Mo lowered his head, shaking it, then put his hands in his front pockets.

"My immorality!" I screamed, pulling the covers up to my chin. "There's nothing immoral about me!"

"This is disgraceful! We have a respectable house." Rasha screamed.

"I'm respectable," I yelled back.

"This is my home!" Rasha yelled. "You need to leave! You've soiled my house!"

Mo nodded. "You need to leave."

Sarah also nodded.

"Don't worry. This evil presence is leaving your home," I shot back. "I don't want to hang around with all this religious junk!"

"Our religion!" Mo bellowed. "You know nothing about our religion."

"I shall break a clay pot behind her!" Rasha yelled. "I need to cleanse this house!"

The screeching trio surrounded me. I cowered on the sofa, pulling the blanket up to my ears to block some of the yelling. It felt like the Seboa all over again, them taking turns to out-shout each other in Arabic.

Amidst the yelling, I heard Yousef calling down from the top of the stairs. "Janelle! I have breakfast!" Then a pause. "What's happening?"

"Yousef!" I screamed. "Help me! Tell them to get out of here!"

Yousef now stood in front of all of us with a paper bag and a tray with two cups of coffee. "What's going on?" Yousef asked.

Yousef yammered away to Mo in Arabic. Mo yelled back in his face. Rasha oscillated between yelling at me, then Yousef, then me again, never giving her waving arms a break. Sarah was weeping, alternating between clasping her hands and holding them up to God.

Yousef set down breakfast, then collapsed in the chair. He hung his head. Rasha yelled at him one last time, then stormed out of the room. Sarah followed her.

Mo said in English, in a comment that was clearly intended for me to hear, "I never expected you to do this. You've completely dishonored and disrespected us."

Mo then trailed after Rasha and Sarah.

"Where is the disrespect? He's my boyfriend," I yelled.

"My God, help me," Yousef said. "What has happened?"

"What do you think happened?" I bawled. "They came down and saw me naked. Sarah comes down with your breakfast—what's that all about—and finds me. She screams, drops the food, and they come running. What do you think happened?"

"Janelle, I'm so sorry," he said, joining me on the sofa, attempting to hug me.

"You're sorry? They didn't even know I was here!" I said, pushing him away from me. "What am I to you? Your dirty little secret? Are you embarrassed by me?"

"Janelle, it's not that."

"Then what is it?"

"My family," he said. "You don't understand."

"I thought I was your family!" I screeched. I flung off the blanket and hurled a string of expletives at him as I put on my clothes. "You're unbelievable. You're not the person that I thought you were. You didn't even stick up for me. You coward. You loser."

"It's not what you're thinking. I just needed some time to tell my family."

"I was just a secret in Mo's basement. Nobody knew about me, did they?"

"I'm trying to balance my culture, family, and you. They were upset."

"They were upset?" I said, collecting my toiletries and clothes, and shoving them into my backpack. "What about me? I'm the one who was naked in front of a bunch of Arabs, with my boobs hanging out for everybody to see. I come first, Yousef. We talked about having a life together. I come first in that life, not your cousin."

I didn't wait for him to respond. "And what was Sarah doing down here, anyway? Giving you food early in the morning?"

"Janelle—"

"Stop it, Yousef," I said. "She speaks English. That stupid little bitch speaks English. But the entire night, she didn't talk to me at all. Did you know she speaks English?"

"We all learn English," he said.

"So why didn't she talk to me?" I said, putting my backpack on and grabbing my helmet. "Are you lining her up to be your wife instead of me? Keeping me around for fun?"

"Janelle, it's not like that at all. You mean so much to me. You're number one."

"And she's number two? She's your second wife? Is that how it works, Yousef? You really didn't leave those traditions behind, did you?"

"Janelle, she's my cousin."

"You marry your cousins in Egypt!" I yelled, going up the stairs.

Yousef followed me. "I have no feelings for her. She's like a sister."

"What about her konafa? I see how you drool all over her," I said, tilting my head, flicking my eyelashes, and accenting my words in mimicry of Sarah, "Yousef, some konafa for you?"

"Janelle, please, her konafa means nothing to me. You mean everything to me."

"Does your family want you to marry her? Is that it? Don't think I'm stupid, Yousef. I can see it in her eyes—and yours."

"It doesn't matter what my family wants," he pleaded.

"Wrong answer," I said. "So you do love her. You're not willing to stand up to your family for me?"

I reached for the door handle, but Yousef stretched his arm across the doorframe to block my exit. I karate-chopped his arm and went through.

"Ow!" he said, holding his hurt arm. "Janelle, please! I love you."

"Goodbye Yousef. Enjoy your breakfast."

***

I stood in the bathroom mirror, looking at my destroyed self. As upset as I was about the breakfast I made Yousef fly in the air, I knew Rasha was even more upset. Down the hall, Mo was consoling my sister, who hadn't stopped crying about how her house was soiled with immorality.

Some of the breakfast food had already begun to dry onto my hijab and galabeya. Bits of fried egg and beans hung on, leaving stains as I scraped them off. Big stains. Small stains. Dark stains. Light stains.

Now I'm stained. I was moving toward possible marriage with a man who wasn't honourable and didn't respect our traditions. Yousef was having a secret relationship with a Western woman. The kind of Western woman who didn't have morals. I suppose I shouldn't have been so surprised, as it happens to many people when they leave Egypt.

I dampened the washcloth and added soap, then scrubbed my clothes. I was becoming intertwined with Yousef, showing my love through my cooking. He missed his mom's cooking so much, and I was definitely stepping into that role of being the woman in his life. He loved my cooking and couldn't keep himself away from it. I knew he loved coming home and finding dinner waiting for him.

When I came to collect the dirty dishes in the morning, barely a mouthful was left in the pot. It was eaten clean like a hungry animal does to a bone, not leaving any evidence of meat once being there. I'd laugh at how clean it was and imagined him sitting at the kitchen table after work, studying for his pharmacy exams, eating my food and scraping the dish until nothing was left.

Now, I'm scraping my food off my hijab and galabeya. What a bitter joke that has been played on me. All this time, he was having a secret relationship with another woman. But why that kind of woman? Yousef came from a good family. His father was well-established in the community and his family was good.

120

And he did it in my sister's house. That's what I can't get over. If you're going to have a relationship with a woman like Janelle, why soil your cousin's house? My God. Please forgive this man and all of who he really was. I can never be with a man like that. Maybe Canada changed Yousef.

Rinsing the washcloth, I wiped my face, not because there was any food left on it, but to wipe away my tears.

My future in Canada with Yousef was definitely over. I adjusted my hijab, concealing the strand of hair that poked out. I'll put these clothes in the laundry, but first I need to talk to Rasha.

In the kitchen, Rasha and Mo sat at the table having tea. The baby was on Rasha's lap, feeding. The children were nearby, carrying some books under their arms pretending they were in school today. Rasha was good about getting the kids into reading at a young age.

"Sarah," Rasha said, "Please sit down and have some tea. Calm yourself."

I joined them, placing a sprig of mint into the glass and pouring the tea over top. The tea covered the mint, submerging and overwhelming it.

"Rasha, my dear sister," I said, "I see you're now managing the baby and doing well. You don't need me here anymore."

"What are you talking about?" Rasha erupted.

Mo placed his hand on her shoulder, soothing her.

"Of course I need you. The baby is only a few days old. What will I do without you? Who will help me with all the children? Cook? Sarah, please don't leave. You're such a big help to us."

"I don't feel I belong here," I said, tears trickling down my face. "I have this enormous feeling of homesickness. I see how Canada is beautiful and people here live a good life and well-taken care of, but I miss Egypt."

"We all miss Egypt," Rasha said. "But Egypt is not everything. Sarah, think about the life you can have here."

Yousef flashed through my mind. "Rasha, I miss the crowds, the busy streets, the sleepless alleys and the people with their bad and good," she said. "I belong there, not here."

In my sister's sudden and prolonged silence, I knew that she understood, and would stop trying to convince me. "I'm going home."

CHAPTER 19

I could barely focus on my work at the casino. I didn't know what was worse. Being naked in front of a group of strangers or Yousef keeping me a secret for almost six months.

I'd had the highest hopes for our relationship. I knew that Yousef wouldn't cheat on me like Daniel did. I knew he wouldn't screw and dump me like the others did. But keeping me a secret was really the worst feeling of all.

I scrolled through Yousef's texts that I hadn't returned: was I still mad at him, it would be nice to see me, why don't I call, he's sorry...

I stared at my screen, replaying the entire debacle in my head. Being discovered that way was the ultimate humiliation—that I was his dirty little secret and they were in shock and horror that a woman of such ill repute was contaminating their home. They were the ones who stumbled across me, not the other way around. I didn't go upstairs and prance around naked scaring the kids.

What was I in their eyes, really? Vermin? Something that needed to be exterminated? I could see the women, especially Sarah, running around in their hijabs and galabeyas, spraying everything down that they thought I touched in his apartment. Spraying and praying. Rinse and repeat.

It seemed Sarah was in his basement all the time anyway, trying to seduce him with her cooking and cleaning, all engineered to lure him in. Yousef bragged about her konafa as if it won a gold medal in some international cooking competition. But then again, it was like his mother's, so maybe she was a gold medalist in his mind. Maybe these Egyptian women did know how to get a man, at least one of their own men.

If I didn't increase my productivity, it'd be another reason for my boss to jump all over me. However, fixing customers' computer problems wasn't at the top of my mind.

I found it difficult to shake my feelings. I felt so exposed and vulnerable. I'd finally found a partner who I thought I could rely on and trust. A man who treated me well, and I was on the cusp of being wide-open, emotionally vulnerable with him, placing my heart on the line, and he shattered it. Every time I got close to somebody, something happened, and this time was no different. Even so, I was never in a comparable situation where somebody yelled that I'd dishonored and disrespected their household. If Yousef wouldn't stand up for me at this stage, when would he?

I wanted to delete all of Yousef's emails and texts and be finished with yet another man who didn't value me, but I couldn't bring myself to do it. I loved his texts, the way he thought about me throughout the day—with a bouquet of flowers, two puppies holding a heart between them, and the funny gifs. I couldn't delete him from my life forever.

My phone rang. It was Mom. "Janelle, I heard you came over with your new boyfriend," she said.

I didn't bother to correct her. Maybe he wasn't a new or old boyfriend anymore, but another relationship staggering toward failure like all the others.

"Sorry we didn't see you," I said mechanically.

"Does he speak English? I heard he didn't laugh at any of your father's jokes," she said. "Is he really serious?"

"I don't know anymore," I said.

"That doesn't surprise me. Nothing worked out since you left Daniel," she said. "We all loved Daniel."

My boss wandered by my desk, peering at my screen. I opened an email and pointed to my phone, mouthing "customer" to him. He raised his eyebrows and slunk away.

"Maybe you should get back together with Daniel," Mom said. "Think about it. I know he still loves you."

Mom always had advice, even though it was mostly unwanted and unwarranted, but she was right. It might be easy to get Daniel back, especially since he'd made overtures while Meghan was visiting her parents for the weekend. He turned on the charm he used to have.

"I don't think this Egyptian guy's family is going to be any different. Maybe even worse. Janelle, I don't trust them," Mom confided. "And he's going to change after marriage, believe me, after he gets his hooks into you. You're going down a path of self-destruction. Get back together with Daniel."

She was always so dramatic, like Armageddon was on its way, and it was coming to get me.

"Thanks for your advice," I said. "I'm sorry, but I need to get back to work." These calls with Mom always felt like criticism. I never did anything right in her eyes. Of course it'd have been easier and more convenient to get back together with Daniel, but I needed to work it out with Yousef.

I opened a customer email and categorized the software incident. One by one, I assigned the incidents to the specialist to resolve. If I could only resolve my own issues so quickly and resolutely.

A meeting request for a company-wide meeting appeared in my email. Another boring company meeting. The executives would go on for hours and hours about market share and strategic directions, and all I'd hear was "blah, blah, blah." I followed my coworkers down the hall and all of us sheep seated ourselves. At the front of the room stood my boss and the human resources director.

"Good morning," he said. "There is no way to say this bad news well, so I'll just say it. Our team has been broken into two meeting rooms. There's another meeting going on as we're having this one. This will be a short meeting," he said, glancing at the human resources director.

"A key project was cancelled this year by a major client," he said. "I'm sorry to say that we can't sustain the current level of resourcing. Unfortunately, anybody assigned to that project is being released from the company. We're very sorry," he said.

Nice way to say they just fired all of us.

"Do you have any questions?" I heard the human resources director say in the background, but I'd already tuned out. As a temporary worker, I'd be given two weeks' pay and escorted out of the building immediately after the meeting. I knew the drill. In the computer industry, companies didn't put their intellectual assets at risk from a rogue employee. My computer access would have been disabled while I was in the meeting room. Within a week, my personal belongings would be packed and couriered to me.

As my coworkers filed out, a numbness took over me. The job that I disliked so much had been taken from me. My means of paying my bills and sustaining myself were suddenly gone. The remaining staff around me looked as gloomy as I felt. I grabbed my pink helmet and bag. "We'll keep in touch," we said, not knowing if we would, as we were all escorted out of the building.

I sat on my motorcycle, tears sliding down my cheeks. I wouldn't see the inside of that lousy building anymore, but that shitty place was paying my bills.

I really needed Yousef right now. He was the only person who would listen without criticizing. I needed his kind and uplifting words, his warm embraces. I hadn't heard back from him, yet I knew he always kept his phone nearby. He always responded right away. I texted him.

Sorry I've been AWOL.

He wouldn't know what that meant. I texted again.

Sorry I've been missing.

***

Later that day when I arrived home, I discovered a deposit in my room. And it wasn't a bank deposit. "Pepper! What did you do?" I screamed.

Pepper's pile of shit was sitting on my carpet. Mag appeared in my bedroom doorway. "I heard you screaming like a banshee. I thought somebody died. What happened?"

"Pepper crapped in my room."

I was so distraught I needed to hang onto somebody, even if that somebody was Mag. First, I was fighting with Yousef, then I got fired, and now this. My entire life was turning into a disaster. Even Pepper was against me.

I pointed to the pile near her feet. "I nearly stepped in it."

"That's a big pile. He had a lot to let go," Mag said. "You should open some windows."

"I know, I know. It's disgusting," I said, opening my window fully.

"It doesn't seem like him," Mag said. "But then again, you've been spending so much time away. Maybe he's just upset."

"I've no idea. He's never done this before."

"Maybe you shouldn't leave him alone that much," Mag chided. "I had a cat like that. The cat was so smart. He knew when he was being neglected. He'd pay me back that way. Crapped right on my bed."

"I don't really know. I'm so upset at him."

"Maybe he has a health problem," Mag smirked, then turned around and headed downstairs.

"Mag, what do you mean?" I asked.

She cranked her head toward me. "Nothing really, but at the same time, you never know, do you?"

I knelt beside Pepper's deposit. After walking my dog for years, I knew my dog's crap. Pepper's feces were always smaller than that, and more compact. I ran downstairs. "Mag, my dog never craps like that. Did you do something?"

"You're very strange," Mag taunted, stretching out her words as she chomped a strawberry. "To examine your dog's feces like that. You might want to go to the doctor. Maybe you have a condition."

"I'm serious. I know my dog's crap. That's not it," I said. "Did you feed him ex-lax or some other weird shit?"

"My, my, my," she teased. "You're going crazy, aren't you? You should go to a doctor, a psychiatrist really. You're hallucinating," Mag said, spiraling her forefinger at the side of her head. You've reached the breaking point."

"Mag, go clean it up."

"Or what?" she said, sucking another strawberry.

"Or you'll regret it. I've had it. I'm done with you destroying my stuff, and stealing my food. Pushing me out of this house. I'm done with all of it."

"Crazy. Lunatic. Off-balance," she mocked, enunciating every syllable. She picked another strawberry.

I opened her palm and smashed down on the strawberry. The juice splattered everywhere. "This is what crazy looks like Mag."

Meghan picked up the remnants of the strawberry and threw them at me. I ducked, and it hit the wall behind me. I took another strawberry from the basket, took aim, and tossed it like a baseball, with as much force as needed to reach the outer field. It smacked Mag in the forehead and caused her to step back. As Mag regained her balance, I stepped toward with another strawberry and mashed it into the center of her forehead.

"What a crappy experience, huh, Mag? Looks like you're wearing a beauty masque. It'd certainly improve your looks."

Mag covered her face with her hands, peeling off the bits of strawberry that stuck to her. "Danny! Danny!" She yelled. "Janelle's assaulting me!"

Daniel ran into the kitchen. "What's going on here?" He immediately wrapped his arms around her.

"She threw strawberries at me and hit me in the face," she wailed.

Daniel wiped off her face, soothing her, his arms cocooning her. "Janelle, have you lost your mind?"

"She threw it at me first, but she missed. I happen to have better aim than she does—better everything, actually," I said.

"No, this is insane," Daniel said. "I'm tired of it. This fighting has got to stop. I don't work hard all day to come home to a catfight."

"She did something to Pepper. He crapped in my room, and there was too much."

"Too much? This is nuts. You know what? Why don't we ask Pepper?" Daniel asked, lacing his tone with sarcasm.

I was silent.

"You're absolutely insane," Mag cried, hugging tighter onto Daniel. A tear slowly trickled down her cheek.

I was fed up with her fake crying. What a terrible actor she was.

"Janelle," Daniel said, "You assaulted Meghan. Now you've gone too far. I want you out."

"Assaulted her? Are you serious? We threw strawberries."

"Get out of this house," he said, pointing toward the door. "Get all of your crap out."

"Yeah, Janelle, get your crap out," Mag taunted. "Even the crap upstairs."

Mag's tears had mysteriously disappeared just as real ones were starting in me. I had to maintain my composure. Had to think this through. He can't kick me out right now. I had nowhere to go, no job to pay for a new place, and Yousef wasn't on the radar right now.

"Daniel, I own part of the house. You can't kick me out."

"I'm buying you out. And if you don't want that, then I will sell it. I'm sick and tired of living like this."

Somehow, I don't think this strawberry fight had anything to do with his decision to end our threesome. Strangely, it's happening not long after he met Yousef.

"Where am I going to go? Jesus!"

"Go to Yousef's. I don't care. Go anywhere. Just leave."

"What am I going to do with Pepper?"

"You're not taking him," Daniel said.

"Don't be so heartless!" I screamed. "He's coming with me."

"Where?" Daniel asked. "Just get out."

What the hell would I do? I can't go to my dysfunctional family. Yousef wasn't talking to me. Maybe I could crash on a friend's couch for a while. I had lost my whole fucking life in a blink. And now I have to fight for my best friend, Pepper. Oh, fuck me.

Behind Daniel, Mag sneered, kicked her right leg forward as if kicking a field goal, then raised both hands in victory above her head.

***

I needed to talk to Yousef, even if it meant showing up at his pharmacy with the flimsy excuse to return a T-shirt. I parked my motorcycle in the first spot I saw at the grocery store, ignoring another driver's signal light that claimed it.

My entire world had been ripped apart—I had no job, no home, no Pepper, and it seemed, no Yousef. He hadn't returned my texts, each one I knew more desperate in tone than the previous. Still, I can't appear too desperate, and the excuse of returning his T-shirt might open a door for me back into his life.

I didn't understand. He'd always returned my texts.

"God, Yousef, why are you doing this to me?" I murmured as I ran into the store, T-shirt in one hand and helmet in the other. I ran past the screaming kids, grocery carts jammed in the aisles, and the banana-breakers, the people who painstakingly broke apart banana bunches to create their own.

At the pharmacy, I pushed myself ahead of the long line of customers and flagged down Mo, waving my arms like I was drowning in a pool. "Mo, where's Yousef?"

"Janelle, I have customers," Mo said, speaking past me to the next customer. "Sir, I'm so sorry. How may I help you?"

I placed my helmet and the T-shirt on the counter, separating Mo from his customer. In a louder voice, I demanded, "Where is he?"

"Janelle, please wait until I serve these customers." He slid my helmet and the T-shirt to the side.

Realizing this wasn't an opportune time to be kicked out of the store, I stepped back and checked my texts, but Yousef still hadn't responded. Nor did he send me any emails or voicemails. Customers continued to line up at the pharmacy, making the line even longer, so I tacked myself onto the end.

One by one, Mo greeted customers, accepted their prescriptions or gave them their pills, and wished them a good day. It was now my turn. "Mo, I need to talk to you."

"Janelle, I told you that I have customers."

"I'm a customer," I said, squaring my body to his. "I'm looking for some pharmacy information."

I snatched a package of antacid tablets from the display beside me and slapped it on the counter. "I have a sore throat. Are these the mints you recommend?"

Mo rolled his eyes. "Those are antacid tablets for the stomach. If you have acid."

"I have a sore throat and acid. What do you recommend?"

Mo sighed. "One of the assistants can help you."

"No, I need the pharmacist to help me," I insisted. "This is a serious medical issue."

"Then go see your doctor," Mo said.

"Mo, please tell me where he is. Is he at home?"

Mo shuffled bags of prescriptions around in the basket, as if it was food he didn't want to eat on his dinner plate. "I think it's in your interest as well as his for you to leave him alone. Ever since you came into his life you've caused problems. Rasha and I've both seen that. Yousef is no longer focused on his exams. He's not studying. You've played games with him."

"Mo, I know I've made some mistakes, but Yousef and I love each other. It's not your business to stand in our way."

"If he loves you so much, then why don't you know where he is?"

"Is he at home?"

"Janelle, don't you dare go to my home and scare Rasha," Mo said. "We don't want you around our family."

"Scare Rasha? What about Sarah?" I pried.

Mo stared at me. "You're no longer a threat to Sarah."

"What are you saying, Mo? Why, did Sarah leave? She went back to Egypt, didn't she?"

"Yes, she did, with Yousef," Mo said. "You got the information you're looking for. Now leave this place immediately."

"You did this. All of you did. I was ruining your plan, wasn't I? You never wanted him to be Canadian."

"Janelle, I'm calling security. Go home and forget you even met Yousef."

I knew I had to back off, since I wasn't getting any more information from Mo. I took off down the grocery aisle. "Move! Move!" I yelled, hoping the people would part in a Moses miracle. "This is an emergency!"

I pushed the carts out of the way.

"Hey, lady, watch it!" a man yelled at me.

"I'm sorry, it's an emergency!"

Once outside, I straddled my motorcycle, turned on the ignition, and backed out.

"That's a disability spot!" a woman shouted. "You need a permit!"

"My sign blew away!" I screamed, revving my engine and tearing out of the parking lot.

"Sarah, you hag," I murmured. "You won't take him away from me that easily. You've no idea who you're dealing with. Just wait until I see you."

CHAPTER 20

When the plane landed at Cairo International Airport, I obtained the visa, withdrew money from the cash machine, then stood in line with the other foreigners getting asked the requisite questions. The reason for my visit didn't fit in nicely with the customs landing card. Business? No. Study? No. Culture? No. Medical treatment? No, but it may be later when I find Sarah. So, I picked tourism.

Except for some heavy police presence, the airport was as modern as one in Canada, with passengers flowing through the arrivals and baggage areas. Even the luggage belt was similar, the suitcases going round and round until a passenger rescued it. I had none to save, for in my haste I threw some clothes into a carry-on and ran to the airport. Nevertheless, I never knew Egypt would look like this. Not sure what else I expected. Camels walking around the airport?

With my carry-on rolling behind me, I stepped into the airport convenience store. I needed something to calm my nerves. A crutch, something to help me deal with my anxiety. My hands gravitated toward a package of Cleopatra cigarettes. I despised smoking, but completely understood the habit right now.

I needed a strong woman like Cleopatra by my side to give me the strength to complete my mission in Egypt.

Outside, I sat on a bench already occupied by an older man. His eyes travelled the length of me, from my sweater down to my yoga pants. I moved to the edge of the bench away from him.

I lit a cigarette and inhaled deeply but the smoke got trapped at the back of my throat, causing me to gag and cough. Tried again. This time I sustained the inhale and a sudden rush hit. I held it, then exhaled fully. It was intense, making me dizzy and off-balance. I hadn't smoked since I was a teenager. This was nuts.

It was still hot in Cairo in September, like the hottest of Toronto days. Way too hot for a sweater, which I stuffed into my purse. The man beside me oriented himself towards me and my bare arms, and said in English, "I have a taxi over there, foreigner. I can take you."

"You pig," I said, flicking my hand at him. I wished I knew how to say pig in Arabic, or worse.

"I try," he said, moving to another bench.

I texted Yousef again.

I'm here. Call me.

I waited a moment, then added to the text.

In Cairo. At the airport.

My phone rang. Yousef! Finally. I put out my cigarette.

"Janelle, where are you?"

"I told you. At the airport in Cairo."

"Don't play games with me."

I described the airport and the visa process, and that I was now smoking Cleopatra cigarettes.

"When did you start smoking?" he asked. "Janelle, that's bad for your health."

I ignored the question. At least he was talking to me. "Yousef, I miss you so much. The pain of not having you is unbearable."

"What do you think you're doing? We're having family time right now. I can't do anything for you. I have so much to do. I can't explain right now."

So he didn't get married yet. Good news. But it also meant I had to act fast.

"What do you mean, family time?"

"Don't bother yourself. It's too complicated," he said. "Janelle, I can't talk right now. My Mom needs me."

"Yousef, just share your location with me. The GPS isn't working."

"Why? You're going to follow the blue dot to find me? Just stay at the airport. You need to go back to Canada."

"If you don't share your location, I'll come find you."

"You'd try to find me in the 6th of October City? With three million people?"

"I can find you. I got to Cairo, didn't I? I'll go to the police station and file a missing person's report."

"Janelle, don't you dare go to the police. Not in this country. They're not friendly Canadian police. You don't know what might happen to you."

"Then share your location. Or I'm coming to find you."

"Fine. Here's my location," he said. I switched to the friend finder app and saw Yousef, now a blue blinking dot, in 6th of October City. I immediately took a screenshot of it, just in case Yousef decided to turn himself off again.

"I see you now, thank you," I said.

"Now go back to Canada."

"I can't. I need to see you."

"Janelle, Cairo is no place for you. Go back."

"No."

"You're acting like a child now. Go back to Canada."

"I'm not going until I see you. I'll wait for you."

Yousef sighed. "Do you promise to wait there?"

"I promise," I said. "I promise I'll wait." In my mind, I didn't clarify where I was promising to wait. If I had finished the sentence, I'd have said, "I promise I'll wait for you to get off the phone so I can get in a taxi and find you."

"Stay there," Yousef said. "You promised. I'll be there when I can. It might be a few hours. Don't go outside of the airport."

"I already said I'd wait," I said.

***

I ran back into the airport, finding the universal taxi sign and an attendant sitting at a desk underneath in a white uniform. "Excuse me, do you speak English?"

"How may I help?" he asked.

"I need a taxi." I showed him my phone, where the dot of Yousef blinked. I enlarged the map. "How much does it cost to get here?"

"6th of October City is outside of Cairo near the Great Pyramids. It'd cost four hundred Egyptian pounds."

"How long will it take to get there?"

"It depends on the traffic. Maybe one hour. Maybe two."

I paid my fare at the taxi office, sliding the credit card into the machine. "Credit cards let you be in debt all over the world," I said to the attendant.

He laughed. "Thank you, have a nice day. Enjoy your trip. The taxi is outside. Show him this piece of paper."

All of the dented taxis were lined up outside. It was almost as if you needed to be dented before being allowed to join them. Were the dents a metaphor for life here, a message of getting hit and then getting up and going again? I needed this message right now. I stepped into the next taxi waiting in line and handed the paper to the driver, a man in his fifties with dark hair and a bushy moustache.

"Do you speak English?" I asked.

"How I help you?" the driver responded.

I showed him my screen. "I need to go here," I said, pointing at the blue blinking dot.

"I see it later," he said. "More than one hour."

"My name is Janelle," I said. "What's your name?"

The driver pointed to his taxi card. "Mohammed. Millions of Mohammeds in Egypt. Why are you in Egypt?"

"Vacation," I said.

"By yourself?"

"I'm joining my husband," I said.

Mohammed said nothing as he navigated out of the modern airport highway and into the Cairo traffic, where I was immediately shelled with the sights, sounds, and smells of Cairo. Mohammed jammed his way into the traffic, continually testing and advancing, even if only an arm's length, to gain entry. Cars were so close to each other that I could see the stubble of the driver in the next vehicle. Stoplights didn't seem to have much significance.

I could taste the grit on my teeth and covered my mouth to block out the diesel-filled air. It was gridlock unlike I'd ever seen, even coming from Canada's biggest city. The congestion sprawled out in front of us, thousands of cars bumper to bumper, drivers careening into lanes they made up themselves. The other drivers sometimes honked or shook their fists at each other. I dug my hands into the folds of the backseat in an unsuccessful attempt to find the seat belt as I was tossed from side to side. I gripped the door handle.

Mohammed alternated between honking and flashing his high beams, gliding in and out of lanes. I'd counted five unofficial lanes, but who really knew? None of them were marked. He frequently slowed down along with the other drivers when approaching the massive speed bumps on the highway which scraped the bottom of the taxi.

As we passed rows of gigantic apartment buildings under construction, Mohammed said, "They build new cities. Don't fix the old."

The drivers seemed to continuously avoid near-collisions, testing and pushing, and cajoling and forcing each other into movement that served their purpose. Donkeys pulled carts alongside the cars, being whipped with small, tattered ropes as they transported carts full of fertilizer, tomatoes, or other goods. Drivers in three-wheeled tuk-tuks had more bravado, sneaking in between cars, acting bigger than they were, like bulldogs in a fight but always allowing that bit of leeway to allow the entire system to work. To allow Cairo to work. To allow life to work.

Suddenly I was surrounded by voices coming out of loudspeakers. The soundscape was dominated by these strong and powerful male voices, full of rhythmic eloquence. Even without understanding the words, I was moved by the spiritual feelings swelling inside me. The voices were simultaneously magnetic and captivating, magnificent and authoritative, yet poetic.

Mohammed said, "Call of the prayer. Afternoon prayer. Only the best voices say."

At that moment, I recalled Yousef telling me about these voices from the loudspeakers, the mosques' dueling minarets calling Muslims inside to pray. They were so overwhelming that I could focus on nothing else, and now understood how the rumor started about Neil Armstrong hearing the call of the prayer from the moon, as it seemed to float above the entire city. The beautiful tones soothed my nerves.

"What are they saying?" I asked.

"God is great, God is great. No God except Allah. Mohamed is a prophet of Allah," Mohamed said. "For so many years they call us but now we also have apps on our phones to tell us," he said, holding up his phone.

As the call of the prayer died down, the sounds of Cairo resurfaced, and the horn honking rose up, overtaking the last voice as it dwindled away. Cairo had once again become Cairo. As Mohammed navigated the narrow streets, he kept his hand close to the horn and his foot on the gas.

"The Nile," Mohammed said, as we crossed a bridge.

So this was the famous Nile Cleopatra floated down thousands of years ago. How the Nile had seen Cairo change. I couldn't believe I was passing by and not stopping at the most famous river in history.

As we came around a curve, Mohammed pointed out of his window. The triangular tips were unmistakable in the distance, through the haze of pollution. "The Pyramids," he said.

"I can see that," I said, sticking my head out the window to get a better look. The diesel smell forced me to retreat.

It was unbelievable that I was whizzing past all these archeological wonders of the world as if they were familiar sights. Like I was passing a shopping mall.

"What needs to be discovered is far more than what we know now," I recalled Yousef saying. I always imagined the first time I'd see the Pyramids would be with Yousef. I wanted to see him so badly. Be in his arms.

Vendors lined up in precarious places along the major artery to sell apparently anything—rugs, phones, fruit, smoothies, or animals. They seemed to set up shop in anything, even a shanty, waiting for their customers. Garbage lined the streets where flowers and shrubs could be, and laundry hung out of apartment windows.

When the traffic stopped, children courted the drivers to buy their little trinkets and toys, pleading with their innocent eyes as the adults who minded them waited nearby. There was a strong spirit of survival here. The need to hustle through life was pervasive.

Yet somehow, Cairo seemed to meld together, all the horn honking, loud exhaust pipes, and people calling each other on the street over the traffic noise, beckoning for one thing or another. It was organized chaos.

I hadn't been fair to Yousef. The cars on this highway let each other in better than I had let Yousef into my life. I'd taken the entire road for myself, and left

Yousef into one of the narrow alleyways, making it impossible for him to get onto the road with me. How wrong I'd been. How very foolish and spoiled I'd been. Yousef was the best thing to have ever happened to me.

Yousef had been the opposite of me. He'd been accommodating, letting me in, not worrying about his schedule nor time and place, but giving way to me, making sure I was taken care of.

In the middle of the street, a herd of cows crossed the heavy traffic that obligingly stopped for them as they moved from a tiny patch of grazing land to another. These drivers were more respectful to the cows than I'd ever been to Yousef. What a horrible person I'd been.

A motorcycle passed the taxi, squeezing itself between two cars. The rider navigated the narrow opening without a helmet, wedging a mobile device between his shoulder and face. His female passenger sat in the side saddle position, carrying her baby. Lane splitting was beyond illegal in Canada. I gasped.

Everything in Canada would've been so different for Yousef. I had no idea how much effort he would've had to exert to change, but I kept pushing him, didn't I? Kept accusing him of not being Canadian enough when he hadn't even been in the country for a year.

Yousef had tried so hard to fit into Canadian culture. Yet, I never tried to change for him. Yousef tried to learn all about my culture and be so respectful, and I knew that he used all of his energy and love to adapt to his new home, to become a new person to me. I'd abused his trust and had acted like an overindulged child.

Cairo blended everything together—the good, bad, and the ugly. It was all there, just like life. I couldn't always have my own way. Perspectives weren't so black and white. Yousef wasn't a computer system that turned on and off, run only by logic. I needed to be more flexible and think more about him.

"Are there a lot of accidents?" I asked Mohammed.

"With people? Yes, too many," he said. "We stopped counting."

The apartment buildings had mainly disappeared and we were now on the Alexandria desert highway. The pure desert and an endless view of sand on both sides of the highway led to Oasis Road which took us into 6th of October City, where again the marks of a city cropped up.

As Mohammed continued, the distance between Yousef's blue blinking signal and me was getting much shorter.

"Can I see the screen again?" Mohammed asked. I handed him the phone.

He stopped in the middle of a dirt street. "We're here," he said, looking in his rearview mirror at me. Mohammed pointed at the tent. "Maybe the tent?"

The fabric tent with its peaked roof was erected in front of an apartment building, taking part of the street for itself, near where children played ball.

"Thank you," I said, putting a fifty Egyptian pound tip in his hand.

"Madame, enjoy Cairo."

I ran toward the tent, then stopped in front of it, fully taking it in before I moved one more step. The side that faced me wasn't walled and I had a good view of the inside.

Persian rugs covered the entire ground and ornate wooden armchairs with tall backs, several occupied by men, were lined up in rows. In front of the chairs, a man read aloud from a book. He reminded me of a minister who read during marriage ceremonies. This was probably where the wedding was taking place.

Suddenly, I was afraid to take another step. How could I barge into a private ceremony? This kind of stuff only happened in the movies, where guests were asked if they disagreed with the wedding then somebody coughed and choked on their words. It was ridiculous to think that my life had turned into a movie. But why else was I here, then? It was to take Yousef back to Canada with me.

I charged ahead. "Yousef!" I screamed. "Yousef! Where are you?"

The reader stopped. He looked up, over and past the men listening, then at me. I could feel his eyes burn into my skin through my yoga pants and sleeveless shirt. He gasped. The other men followed his eyes to where I stood and also gasped. I now had the full attention of everybody in the tent. I felt undressed and exposed.

"Yousef!" I called out again.

I froze, unable to lift up a single toe, afraid to enter further. Everybody looked so similar, all with dark hair and eyes, and wearing formal wear. Which one was Yousef? The children outside approached me slowly, pushing each other toward the foreign woman to get a closer look, then ran off.

CHAPTER 21

How life can change in an instant, adversity striking like an Egyptian cobra and its poison venom. One day, I was building my life in Canada; the next day, I was back in Cairo with my family. Just a week ago, I was so happy when Mo told me I got a permanent part-time job in his pharmacy. It was helping me to become independent of my family and give me the work experience I needed. Then, suddenly I was yanked back to Cairo.

My left eye twitches never failed to warn me that something terrible had happened, and it didn't this time, either. Getting the scary news from Dad about Mom's mini-stroke terrified me. I felt so helpless sitting in Canada, not knowing what might happen to Mom. Janelle hadn't been speaking to me, anyway, for a couple of weeks, not that I could blame her. She had a right to be mad at me for keeping her a hidden secret in the basement.

I couldn't stay in Kingston and not be by Mom's side, especially given the quality of Egyptian healthcare. Indeed, Dad would have obtained the best private healthcare, where the doctors were typically Western trained as opposed to the healthcare poor people received. They were often forced to go to public hospitals where senior student doctors performed surgeries as part of their training. At least the poor had another option, that of the local multigeneration herbalists, who were revered for their abilities and very prevalent in the ancient alleys of Old Cairo.

Even so, in a country where officials routinely overlooked quality deficiencies and kickbacks were common, I couldn't think of my dear mom being put at risk in any way and brought a cache of medications and supplies with me from Canada.

I needed to be here in case her situation worsened or was compounded by medication errors. Sometimes doctors dished out medication like candy.

"Your mother is awake now," the housekeeper said, carrying a tray of tea upstairs. "I'm bringing her some tea."

"I'll take the tray, thank you," I said.

Mom was sitting up in bed, propped up by several pillows. I set the tray down on the side table and stirred in the sugar and milk the way I'd watched her for so many years, enough sugar to sweeten and enough milk to lighten.

"Let it cool," Mom said, declining the tea I held up to her.

"How are you feeling?" I asked, sitting on the edge of her bed and holding her hand.

"I'm tired," Mom said. "But I'm fine, Yousef. You didn't need to come home for me."

"Of course I did," I said, kissing her cheek. "I missed you so much. I couldn't sit in Canada wondering how the doctors were taking care of you."

Behind me, Dad said, "She's getting the best care."

"Dad, I know you'd get the best, but I'm a pharmacist," I said. "I want to watch over things."

"It's a mini-stroke," she said. "I'm fine."

"And she'll be back to normal very soon, holding three phones at the same time, talking to everybody," he said.

Mom smiled, then squeezed my hand.

"We should tell him," Dad said to Mom.

Mom looked away and picked up her tea.

"Tell me what?"

Mom's eyes watered and she wiped them with a tissue.

"He's going to find out," Dad said.

"What are you hiding?" I asked.

Mom said nothing, tears sliding down her cheeks.

"My son," Dad said, "We're sorry to tell you this."

Dad sat in the chair facing me, placing his hand on my knee. "We learned your uncle has late-stage pancreatic cancer. Ahmed hid it for a long time, you know him, but now he's so ill and the situation doesn't look good."

"My God," I said, holding back tears. Uncle Ahmed. Dear Uncle Ahmed. My favorite uncle. I needed to stay strong now, not collapse in front of my parents. I needed to show respect for Uncle Ahmed. How could my favorite uncle be dying?

"We're all upset that he hid it, especially Mom. Why wouldn't you tell your own sister? He didn't want anybody to worry about him, but I think the news of it caused your mom's stroke."

"We can't blame him," she said, dabbing at her eyes with a tissue.

"Not blaming, just explaining," Dad said. "I have a right to my opinion."

She sipped some more tea, then laid back on the pillows, closing her eyes.

"How long does he have?" I asked.

Mom said nothing, and Dad shrugged his shoulders. "It's up to God. Not long."

"I'm so sorry to hear this," I said. "I need to see him now. Can you please call the driver?"

***

As the driver fought with Cairo traffic to Uncle Ahmed's apartment, I sat back and closed my eyes. The typical chaotic clatter of honking horns, broken exhaust pipes, and Egyptians calling out to each other settled into a low murmur as I slipped into my thoughts. This was a day that I thought would never come.

Why did Uncle Ahmed keep his cancer a secret? Maybe he even knew he was sick before I came to Canada. I would've delayed my move to spend more time with him. How death cheats us from the relationships we crave the most.

Memories of Uncle Ahmed poured forth, cycling through my mind, from when I was a small boy and Uncle Ahmed would entertain me with stories of America.

While most of my family stayed in Egypt, when Uncle Ahmed was twenty he forged new territory and started his life in New York City, ignoring the pleas of his family to stay next to them. He began washing dishes at a small restaurant, then climbed the ladder to become a chef and operator. He was then hired as head chef at one of the finest restaurants in the city, cooking for top diplomats and Hollywood celebrities. He kept one eye on the food and one eye on the business. Uncle always told me: plan your next move but do your best in the present.

"Uncle," I said to myself, "I listened to you. I pursued my dreams. You taught me so much. Please wait for me."

My phone buzzed with another text from Janelle. I silenced my ringer. I couldn't deal with her right now. After an hour, we'd reached Uncle Ahmed's apartment.

The driver pulled over, and I ran into the apartment. Auntie opened the door, her eyes red and swollen.

"Dear Auntie, I'm so sorry," I said. "I came over as soon as I heard."

"He didn't want anybody to know," she said, leading me down the hall to the bedroom. "He can only see you for a few minutes. He tires easily."

Uncle Ahmed lay in the wood-framed bed piled up with blankets. His eyes flickered open. "Yousef," he said, reaching for me, "Come here."

I sat beside him.

"The last thing I want to see before I go is this sad look on your face. Smile. We're together now, through God's will."

I forced a smile on my face.

"A real smile, please. You know I don't like fake people."

I tried again.

"That's it. I like that one better." Uncle Ahmed winced and held his abdomen.

I could always count on my uncle for jokes. "Uncle, how are you feeling? Do you need anything?"

"People ask me that all day long," Uncle Ahmed said, waving the notion away. "How are things in Canada? I remember how beautiful it is. The CN Tower was the tallest building in the world."

"Uncle Ahmed, life in Canada is beautiful. I can live the life I want to there. Freedom to make my own decisions."

"You're like me," he said. "Yousef, you've always been like me, open to a new way of thinking. In America, everybody comes together, no matter their religion or status. Everybody can have a chance."

"I know, Uncle, and I'm getting mine. I'm going to be a pharmacist again. I hope to have my own pharmacy next year."

"Next year? Yousef, you've always been a hard worker. You're too good for Egypt. What about your other adventures?" Uncle Ahmed managed a big wink and smile.

"Uncle," I said, feeling the heat of embarrassment rise in my face, "I'm not thinking about that right now, although you know Mom, chasing me to get married by lining up all the cousins she knows."

"Typical Egyptian mother," Uncle Ahmed said, aiming his forefinger in the air, then flinching, and placing his hand on his abdomen again.

"Keep it a secret from Mom, but I met a Canadian lady that I'm quite fond of."

"You can be sure that your secret is safe with me," he said. "So my nephew fell in love. Is she Egyptian?"

"Canadian."

"Is she white? That will help lighten up the race and improve the family genes." Uncle Ahmed said, laughing heartily.

"I'm not sure the family would think so," I said.

"Yousef, I'm at the end of my life, but when I was in America I fell in love with an American. I should have followed my heart. I still think about her," he said. "Not that I'm complaining. I have a wonderful wife who my family introduced me to. She gave me four beautiful children." His eyes cast downward. "But we don't get a second chance at true love, Yousef."

Auntie returned carrying a tray of tea and sweets.

"Yousef, go to Canada. Be with your wonderful woman. Live your life from your heart, not these old customs that don't have any meaning for you."

"Uncle, thank you so much for this. You're the only one who has understood me and given me support."

"Don't worry about them," he said. "They'll figure out their own problems."

Uncle Ahmed closed his eyes.

Auntie moved past me and adjusted her husband's blanket, nodding at me, telling me that my time with Uncle was almost over. Perhaps he needed to sleep.

I held Uncle Ahmed's hand. It wasn't so long ago that I thought of life as days dragging on as years. Now with my ailing Uncle, life had gone the other way, and I measure it in days, soon to be minutes, then seconds.

This might be the last time I see him, and I hoped to absorb as much of him as possible. Uncle Ahmed really understood me and my dreams that had been dismissed by my family. Underneath my family's playfulness was an intent to keep me entrenched in a culture to which I didn't belong. Uncle was the only family member who understood this, for he'd broken away himself decades before I did.

Auntie again nodded at me.

I was reluctant to let go of Uncle Ahmed's hand, as if letting his hand go meant letting go of all of his love, support, and adventurous spirit, and admitting that fate would soon take him.

As I rose from the bed to leave the room, and kissed his forehead lightly, Uncle Ahmed opened his eyes for a moment and winked at me.

***

My cousin told me that only two days after I had visited Uncle Ahmed, he was transferred to the hospital, where he died. I would never hear his laugh again, see his smiling eyes, or be teased by him.

I pictured Uncle Ahmed lying in the hospital bed, taking his last breath in front of my cousin. As his oldest son, my cousin would have closed his father's eyes and summoned the hospital staff to begin the body washing. He would have started the notification process to family and friends.

It was difficult to think of his body, lifeless and without the breath given by God, handed over to a body-washing attendant. Uncle Ahmed would have been washed three times with warm soap and water using only the right hand, then wrapped in three unsewn white cotton cloths, sprinkled with perfumes, and covered with a shawl.

My aunt and other women would have begun their deep mourning, turning on the radio and letting soothing verses of the Quran broadcast throughout the apartment, then praying, asking Allah to have mercy and help the soul leave.

The body was transferred from the hospital to the mosque for noon prayer, which made Uncle Ahmed's death more solid for me. In front of the simple wooden casket, I stood along with the other men in honor of the man who the Imam said was a good servant of Allah. Standing instead of sitting to show him honor.

After the prayer, male family members walked behind the funeral car to the graveyard. My cousins removed the shawl and placed the cotton-wrapped body reverently into a grave, head facing Mecca. One of my cousins put a mud brick under the head, elevating it to the sleeping position.

Men threw handfuls of sand onto the body and blocked the grave, then the Imam recited the opener of the Quran.

The Imam said, "O servant of Allah, if the two angels of the grave ask you who is your Lord, say Allah. If they ask you who is His messenger say Muhammed. If they ask you what is your religion say al-Islam. If they ask you what is your book, say our al-Quran."

On the walk back home, I checked my phone and saw more texts from Janelle. This wasn't the right time to talk to her. I needed to be here for my family. But then she sent a text I couldn't ignore. She was at the Cairo airport. What the hell was she doing! Was this even true? I called her.

"Janelle, where are you?"

"I told you. At the airport in Cairo."

"Don't play games with me."

She described the airport and the cigarettes she was smoking. She'd never know these details unless she was actually sitting right there. Oh my God! I can't talk to her right now. I just need her to stay at the airport until we finish the funeral.

But now she's threatening to come find me. I made her promise to stay at the airport. Janelle is so naïve about Cairo. I didn't need this load on top of everything else right now.

At home, I stood inside the male mourners' tent with my father, uncles, and cousins, sitting in rows of chairs facing each other as the reciter chanted the Quran into a microphone that could be heard throughout the neighborhood.

Hundreds of male mourners worked their way through the rows all day, offering condolences to the family, shaking each hand and saying, "May the rest of your father's life be added to yours."

One of my cousins responded, "May your life last longer."

"Consolidate your strength," another mourner said.

"Strength is given by Allah," another cousin responded.

"May Allah have mercy on your uncle and let him enter His wide paradise," a mourner said.

"Praise Allah," I responded.

We continued to receive the stream of mourners who passed through the tent and the women did the same in the apartment.

Suddenly, the reciter stopped chanting the Quran and gasped in astonishment as he stared at the doorway. All the men turned around to see what had caused such an abrupt interruption and gaped in disbelief at a white woman dressed in tight black pants and a sleeveless shirt, yelling into the crowd. I held my head in my hands. *Oh, my God. I know that voice. What's Janelle doing here?*

CHAPTER 22

As Yousef strode towards me, looking aghast and bewildered and anything but a thwarted bridegroom, I realized that I'd interrupted something very different from Yousef's wedding.

Yousef seized my elbow, squeezing hard, and said, "Let me take you to the women."

He led me out of the tent into a nearby apartment. I wondered what the women were going to do to me.

"Yousef, I came all the way here to see you. I thought you'd be happy to see me. I thought you were—"

"This is my uncle's funeral," he shouted, cutting me off. "You were in the men's tent. No woman is allowed there. You completely humiliated me and dishonored my family."

"You're not getting married to Sarah?"

Yousef froze, fury giving way to astonishment. "Getting married to Sarah? Janelle, what the hell are you talking about? Is that why you're here? And look how you're dressed."

He pointed to my yoga pants and shirt.

He said, "Like a ... like a...."

He briefly glanced around at the few women who were now noticing us. Disgust was written into every line of his face as he looked up at the ceiling and wailed, "My uncle, I'm so sorry."

Tears streamed down my face. "Yousef, I came from Canada to see you. You weren't answering my texts. I didn't know where you were. I missed you so much, but you completely ignored me. I thought you broke up with me and were marrying Sarah."

"Broke up with you?" Yousef yelled. "I left because my mom had a stroke. Then my uncle died."

"I'm so sorry, Yousef, I didn't know. Mo didn't tell me."

"Didn't Mo tell you my mom was sick?"

"He said you went back to Egypt with Sarah, and I should forget about you. I thought you'd left forever," I said, sobbing uncontrollably. "Yousef, I got fired, kicked out of Daniel's house, and lost you. My entire life fell apart. And worst of all, you were gone from my life forever."

"You got fired?"

"The customer ended the contract," I said. "Happens all the time. I guess I wasn't fired, but it sure felt like it. And then Daniel kicked me out because of Meghan." I wiped the tears from my face.

"I know that I've been selfish, Yousef. I understand how much you changed for me. I mean, I saw donkeys on the side of a highway in Cairo. Everything is so different here. Now it looks like I've destroyed everything at your uncle's funeral. Oh my God, what have I done?"

Several women gathered around us, whispering to each other and watching and listening to everything. I didn't want a bloody show. I just wanted Yousef.

An older woman dressed in a long black dress with long sleeves came from behind Yousef. She and Yousef exchanged a few words in Arabic. He seemed to try to reason with her, plead with her somehow. She stepped past him, took my hand, put it in his, and spoke quietly to him. She cried as she spoke, and it hushed the growing crowd of women starting to gather to discover what was going on.

Yousef dropped his eyes to the ground at the woman's words. He held onto my hand even tighter.

"Janelle, my auntie says she's now a grieving widow without a husband but I'm a man who has a woman who loves me enough to follow her heart from Canada."

His eyes welled up with tears. "My uncle would be ashamed if he knew I was so angry at you for loving me this way. My aunt says I must not give up on love so easily because true love is rare and precious. She wishes she'd have the chance to relive the love she's lost."

Yousef's aunt held my hand as she continued to speak to Yousef.

"She said that any woman who comes this far for a man will be a good wife. You'll support me," Yousef said. "She told me that I have her blessing, along with my uncle's."

Yousef took my hand. "Janelle, I'm so sorry. I was taken by so much surprise and so much was going on. I love you more than anything. Even in her grief, my wise aunt has made me realize how precious love is. I'm so sorry." Yousef embraced me.

"I do love you, Yousef. I love you so much," I said, clinging to him. "I want to be your wife. I want to support you in everything that you do."

***

I folded my yoga pants and sleeveless shirt and put on my new orange tunic and jeans, which covered my elbows and flowed loosely over my hips. This would be more acceptable to Yousef's family. He was right about this. "When in Rome," I mumbled to myself.

I knocked lightly on Yousef's bedroom door, opening it slowly. "Yousef, do I look alright?"

"You look wonderful," he said, giving me a morning hug. "I'm glad you bought it."

"I was surprised that I could find jeans at the mall."

"What else would there be?" he teased. "Cairo is an international city. Your dad would be happy to hear there's one-thousand-year-old Christian churches."

"Oh God, don't talk about my dad right now. He'd be horrified if he learned that I'm here. What a fiasco! He'd think that I really did go crazy and have me sent to an asylum."

"They're waiting for us downstairs for the breakfast. Are you ready?"

"Are you sure your parents are okay with me now?" I asked, following Yousef.

"My aunt loves you for coming all the way from Canada to find me. She thinks it's remarkable," Yousef said. "Everybody else is fine. Let's go downstairs and see my parents and sister."

"Yousef, how long will we stay here with your family? Not that I have anything to go back to."

"A few more days. Why do you ask?"

"I'm a bit uncomfortable staying in your parents' home. I guess we can't share a bedroom, but why don't we go to a hotel? We can see them every day."

Yousef led me down the stairs. "We need to show our marriage license when we check in, just in case the police come around." Yousef stopped on the stairway and turned toward me. "We're starting our life together, right?"

"Yes, we are."

"We know each other very well now, right? We enjoy each other."

"All of the above," I said.

"Are we ready to get engaged?"

I hugged him. "My God, I'm so surprised. I didn't expect this."

"Is that a yes?"

"I'd love that."

"It's settled then. Let's go have breakfast and tell the family."

"Yousef, when would we—"

"Come on, my dear, let's share the good news." Yousef grabbed my hand and led me to the breakfast room. His mom and dad and sister were already seated, drinking tea.

Yousef's dad smiled at me and extended his hand, inviting me to sit down. He spoke in Arabic to Yousef, and Yousef translated.

"He says good morning and hopes you had a good sleep."

"Thank you, I did," I said.

As the family helped themselves to the food, Yousef served me and chatted in Arabic with his family.

"Janelle, Dad wanted to know about you, so I told him you have a big house in Toronto, you're an established computer professional, and you come from a loving family."

"Did you tell him about the motorcycle?" I teased.

"Not yet. One thing at a time," Yousef said. "Right now, I'm telling them we're getting married."

"Motorcycle?" his sister asked, simulating handlebars with her fists.

Yousef said firmly, "Not now." She looked down at her plate. He then turned toward his parents and spoke Arabic.

His family broke into a cheer and clapped their hands. His parents and sister took turns interrupting each other, their hands waving in the air to assist in their break-in.

"What are they saying?" I asked.

"They're so excited, Janelle. I can't believe it," he said. "They're wondering if we'll have it in Egypt and what it'll be like. I said of course it'll be in Egypt. We'll have it as soon as everything can be arranged. And of course, Mom says, Janelle will need a beautiful dress for a beautiful bride. She can't wait to plan it for you."

"Plan it for me? Really? I don't plan my own wedding?"

"Yes, really," Yousef said. "Don't worry about a thing. Mom has been through dozens of Egyptian weddings. She knows what to do and will take care of everything."

"What do you mean everything? What are you saying?"

"There'll be five hundred people, at least. Maybe two singers and a DJ, and a belly dancer. And a big buffet. We need good food because that's what people talk about after the wedding. Mom knows the dressmaker and can start the preparations."

"Yousef, I think we should slow down."

"It's ideas right now, my dear," Yousef said. "Mom said we can have a big entrance and a long royal walkway decorated with flowers."

I smiled at Yousef's family. I hope they didn't know it was strained. I felt like my face would crack like the veins in dry clay. Neither of us was prepared financially for a big wedding. "Yousef, this sounds really expensive."

"Don't worry about a thing. It's the groom's family who pays for the wedding."

"It sounds extremely lavish, like a huge party."

I would be happy to get married at the beach with a few friends. Or a small gathering at our home.

"Yes, it'll be a huge party. Egyptians party all night, sometimes until seven in the morning."

"I might be sleeping at my own wedding," I said, picking at my eggs.

"You won't be. The band will keep you awake all night," he laughed.

"Yousef, could we talk about this by ourselves?"

He wasn't getting it at all. Oh God.

"In Egypt, weddings are a family affair," Yousef said. "Everybody gets involved in the big celebration. This is your new family, Janelle."

Is this what my new family was going to be like? So interfering.

"I'm not a flashy person," I said. "I'm a yoga 'Om' person, you know that. If we got married in the forest, that'd be good for me."

"Don't worry, Janelle," he said. "Lots of Egyptian weddings are outdoors. In the desert, we don't need to worry about rain or snow."

He translated this to his family, and they laughed along with him. "An outdoor wedding it is," he said. "Don't worry. We'll talk about everything. They can plan it while we're in Canada, and then we can come back to get married."

Yousef flipped back into Arabic. It seemed that my life was being decided for me. Was I ready for this?

CHAPTER 23

After a couple of weeks in Cairo, it was nice to be back in Kingston. The cool September air was nipping at me, just like when I first arrived in Canada earlier this year, and I pulled up my collar. Did I just say 'nipping'? I was becoming more Canadian by the day. When I encountered Mo in the coffee shop, his half-open eyes gazed tiredly into his cup.

"Salam, Yousef," he said. "Nice to see you back."

"I'm sorry I'm late, Mo," I said, sitting down. "Since we came back, there's so much to do."

"Look at you, acting like a Canadian. Apologizing for your Egyptian time. In Egypt, nothing changes, but life gets behind in Canada when you leave it, doesn't it?"

"I'll tell you in a second, but first, how is Rasha doing? And the children?" I asked.

"Rasha and the children are doing very well. The baby lifts his head now and follows us with his eyes."

"It doesn't take long," I said.

"He's the boss right now. He tells us when to sleep and when to feed him. I forgot how tiring a new baby can be." Mo sipped his coffee. "How are things?"

"Everything is good, Mo. Beyond what I ever could have expected. Egypt revived our relationship."

"I heard. Your Mom called Rasha. So you're getting married?"

"Soon, I'm planning it now," I said. "That's why I was late. There's so much to do."

"I have to admit, I was surprised when I found out. I thought you and Janelle were just … you know … but getting married? If you're sure, Yousef. Marriage isn't easy. You don't have your pharmacy license yet. I've been married for many years, and all I'm saying is it won't be easy."

"Life isn't easy, but it's better with the person you love," I said.

Mo sipped his coffee. "Yeah, that's true. I don't know what I'd do without Rasha."

I laid my hand on Mo's shoulder. "There have been many misunderstandings over the past few months. Isn't it funny how much we've changed since we came here? And you've been in Canada many more years than me."

"Change isn't always good," Mo said.

"I definitely understand," I said. "But some traditions are really meant to die, aren't they? For progress—like human rights and women's rights."

"Most definitely. I'm so glad that Rasha and the kids are here. Did I tell you that the kids are taking hockey lessons?"

"What? Hockey??"

Mo shrugged. "They're Canadian kids. This is what they wanted to do."

"What does Rasha think about this?"

"Surprisingly, she's okay with it. It was Rasha who told me to register them."

"You're kidding me. I never thought I'd hear that from Rasha."

"It's progress. We're in Canada," Mo said.

"Next thing you'll be taking out the garbage."

Mo looked up from his coffee. "The next thing happened already."

I laughed. "I can't believe it."

"I think she saw the neighbors doing it for their wives, so now it's my job, too," he said, examining his empty cup. "Rasha told me it was my new job."

"Mo, I never thought Canada would change you that much."

"It's also my garbage. When Sarah left, everything was too much to take care of, especially with the baby."

Mo leaned in. "You're not going to believe it, but I'm also helping with the cooking. She calls me Mr. Onion Man. As soon as I step into the kitchen, she hands me an onion and a knife and tells me how big to cut it. She got tired of crying," he laughed. "Now I know the difference between dicing and mincing."

I guffawed. "Mr. Onion Man. That sounds like your job for life. To be honest, Mo, I enjoy cooking with Janelle. We're learning together and it's something that we're sharing. It never made sense to me that I sat in the living room while she's alone in the kitchen doing something for me. You know what I mean?"

"Believe me, Mr. Onion Man understands. I don't play soccer online anymore while she's stuck in the kitchen. We're on the same team now."

"Janelle and I are on the same team," I continued. "Sarah is a nice girl, but she never meant anything to me. I know you were trying to look out for me and help Mom, but I never had any interest in my family choosing my wife."

I said, "Mo, that was difficult for me. You're not only my cousin but also my best friend. I know you were following my family's wishes for my marriage."

Mo's face suddenly filled with guilt.

"Yousef, I understand. I think I was trying to do something good for you, but it was misguided. I'm your older cousin and I landed in Canada first. I wanted the best for you. I can see now that you can handle things yourself and in your own way."

"Mo, when I was in Egypt with Janelle, it reaffirmed my decision to live life my way, not my family's way," I said. "It makes me happy."

"Then I'm happy for you," Mo said.

"I have some other good news. Janelle can't keep living with her friend, so she found an apartment for us. We're moving in together."

"Moving in? That's a surprise!"

"I thought we'd marry first, but it'll take some time to plan the wedding and we want to be together."

"When are you moving?"

"Soon," I said. "I hope that's okay. Over the next week. It was rather lucky that she found an apartment."

"I understand this is what you want. If I came to Canada unmarried, I might've done the same," Mo said.

"Life changes us, doesn't it?" I asked.

"I wish you the best," Mo said. "I'm sorry about interfering in your life."

"Mo, don't worry about it. You were doing what you thought was best," I said. "Now Janelle and I will have our life together."

"Thanks to God."

"Mo, would you mind speaking to Rasha? I think she'll understand more if you speak to her. About us moving in together and getting married."

"Sure, no problem. I understand. What are you and Janelle doing this weekend?"

"Not much," I said, "but we're getting ready for Thanksgiving. Janelle was really excited about making a turkey for us. Well ... it's a tofu turkey."

Mo laughed. "No dead birds in her house. How do you find that? Not having meat? Egyptians like to have meat as much as they enjoy breathing."

"Blessings from God, yes," Yousef said, nodding. "She introduces me to a lot of different food. I don't eat vegan all the time, but it's interesting to try new food." I said. "We're also going to have pumpkin pie and pumpkin lattes. Janelle likes pumpkin a lot."

"I can see that," Mo said, smiling.

"Are you and Rasha celebrating Thanksgiving?"

"I'm not sure," Mo said. "We haven't done that before. Isn't it a religious holiday?"

"It's everybody's holiday. Not religious," I said. "Why don't you come over for dinner?"

"Are you sure Janelle wouldn't mind?" Mo asked. "Our entire big family with four children? We'd run you down."

"I've already asked her. Come on over. You've fed me for almost a year. If you don't mind tofu turkey, then come over."

"Thank you, we will."

"Be a Canadian," I teased. "Ask Rasha first."

***

"I wonder if they'll like me this time?" I asked, holding the tattered screen door open for Janelle while balancing the Christmas gifts in the other. Her parents still hadn't fixed the torn screen door from last summer. I'm glad that we're only here for dessert. I'm not sure I could deal with a full Janelle family dinner yet. Food fight? Throwing wine at each other? Endless insults?

"I'm sure they will," Janelle said. "It's Christmas, after all. Even the worst fighters and haters put everything aside at Christmas to love each other," she said, putting her hand on my shoulder. "Or at least they pretend to. Don't worry. My mother is there, which calms my father right down. He's as harmless as a fly around her."

"I hope so," I said.

"Don't worry about it. Everything will be fine," Janelle said. "As much as our family had the huge drunken family brawls, somehow we always managed to put the fighting aside at Christmas. We put on our fake faces and always get through it without pie being thrown at anybody."

Janelle knocked on the door. Footsteps shuffled towards us. I wondered if it would be her dad, sizing me up and ridiculing me again. I loved Janelle and wanted to spend the rest of my life with her but was glad that she only saw her family a couple times a year.

The door opened, and a woman about Mom's age with greying hair and a petite frame appeared. She was wearing red stretch pants and a blue sweater.

"Hi, Mom. How are you? Merry Christmas."

"Merry Christmas, Janelle," she said, "You must be Yousef. I've heard so many good things about you from Janelle. Look at all those gifts you brought. Come on in," she said.

Janelle whispered, "This is a good start."

"It sure is," I said. We followed Janelle's mom into the house. I stepped onto the clean floor.

"It's a shame you couldn't come for dinner," her Mom said. "Anyway, that's fine. I know you're vegan. Come upstairs and see your father. Your brother is serving dinner at the homeless shelter tonight."

A green Christmas tree stood in the corner of the living room, decorated with lights and shiny balls, and an angel on top. Janelle took the gifts from my arms and placed them under the tree.

Janelle's dad rose from his chair. His hair was flattened on his head, combed, and he wore a clean shirt. There were no beer bottles around his chair and the old yellowed newspapers had been cleared away. Christmas really does change things.

"Yousef, Merry Christmas," Janelle's dad said, extending his hand and smiling.

I thought it was an authentic smile, but would he yank my arm off again? Twist it around and cause me pain? After a moment, my hand involuntarily went up. "Merry Christmas, sir. It's so nice to see you."

"It's nice to see you," he said. "It's Harry. You can call me Harry."

Harry gestured to the sofa. "Would you like something to drink?"

The sofa was clean. I could actually sit on any part of it. Partly shocked that this kind gentleman was the same man, I sank my body onto the sofa.

"Water would be fine, thank you."

"I guess you've never had alcohol, now that I think about it," Harry said, shuffling toward the kitchen. "If you ever did, you'd be such a cheap drunk."

Janelle rolled her eyes.

"But that's the healthier option, that's for sure," Harry said. "Good for you. Janelle always liked the liquors when she was a teenager. I used to sneak them to her when her mother wasn't looking."

"I still like them," Janelle said. "Especially the Irish cream. Do you have some of that?"

"Of course," Harry said, disappearing into the kitchen and returning with two glasses.

"I didn't give you vodka, Yousef. It's okay," he said, grinning. "Yousef, I'm a bit of a hard-boiled egg at first. It takes me a bit to take off my shell. And then my back pain, my knees blown out, my arthritis. You just came on a bad day the first time. Sorry about that."

"He's just falling apart, and it shows in his personality," her Mom called from the kitchen. "I'll have some sweets out in a minute."

"Change is harder when you get old. When we were kids we lived on the farm. Life was hard. Nobody had cars, not even motorcycles," he said, winking at Janelle. "Anyway, it takes a while for an old coot like me to get used to change."

"Yousef, would you like some sweets?" her Mom asked, placing them in front of me on the coffee table. "I thought you might like to try real Canadian sweets. I bought Nanaimo bars and butter tarts for you."

This is what Mom would do, treat her guests with honor deserving of the best sweets.

"Nanaimo is a city in British Columbia," Janelle said. "They're good. Chocolate on the outside and crème in the middle. Butter tarts are sweet. Yummy."

"It sounds delicious, thank you," I said, taking a bite of a Nanaimo bar. It was good.

"What do Muslims do on Christmas Eve?" Harry asked.

Janelle cut in. "It's a regular day for them Dad, but Yousef and I went to church service."

"You don't say," Harry said. "You can do that?"

"Of course," I said. "Muslims believe in Jesus. Besides, Janelle loves the choir services at Christmas."

"We used to take her there," her mother said. "I guess it got into her blood."

"It was fun to experience a Canadian Christmas," I said, taking another bite of the Nanaimo bar. "In Egypt, the Coptic Christian service is different. Nice also, of course."

"Coptic Christians were the first Christian church," Janelle said.

"I was seeing something about that on National Geographic," Harry said. "After you were here last time, I came across a lot of shows about Egypt's culture and history. Tommy and I watched them together. It was fascinating. All about the Pharaohs, their medicine knowledge. Society."

"Egypt's history is very fascinating," Janelle said. "Cairo is really fascinating, too. I was there recently."

"You were?" Janelle's mother asked.

"I met Yousef's family. They're absolutely lovely people and were very warm toward me. They've given our relationship their blessing."

"Have you got your stuff out of Daniel's house?" Harry asked.

"I did, a while ago."

"That's probably best," Janelle's mother said. "Get on with your lives. Now that I've met you, Yousef, I can see what a fine person you are. And Janelle said you're a pharmacist, helping people all day long. That's wonderful."

"Pharmacy assistant, for now," I said.

"You watch any hockey?" Harry asked.

"Janelle makes me watch hockey. Does that count?"

Harry laughed heartily, holding his belly. "Yeah, my little girl is a strong one, isn't she? How are you dealing with her?"

"I like and love who she is," I said, smiling at Janelle. In a small, odd way, I felt part of this family tonight.

"It's getting quite late, and we want to get back to Kingston before the snow falls," Janelle said.

"Thanks to both of you for coming out. I know it's a long drive," Harry said.

"A few hours," Janelle said.

"We appreciate it," her Mom said. "And it's so nice to meet you, Yousef."

"Merry Christmas to you," her father said, shaking my hand.

Outside, Janelle turned to me and said, "That wasn't so bad, was it? Now both of our families are on board. Christmas is always the best time to break big news, no matter what it is. It's the only time you're guaranteed a smile."

"Is he nicer to me this time because your mom is here?" Men are always a bit softer when women are around. "I'm still in shock that he was so different."

"It's the Christmas spirit," Janelle said. "Somehow it got inside of him."

I wiped the imaginary sweat off my forehead with the back of my palm and flicked it onto the snow. She laughed and grabbed my hand.

CHAPTER 24

"Are you sure you want to do this?" I asked, as we strapped on our snowshoes. "Snowshoeing is way harder than hiking. Of course I love Frontenac Park but going to the pub would've been a lot easier."

"Our first New Year's Eve should be special," Yousef said. "Recharge in nature."

"I could recharge on a snowmobile, too," I said, leaning down and tightening Yousef's strap. "It needs to be secure so it doesn't fall off. Sometimes these rental shoes aren't the best. A bit worn out with loose straps."

"Besides, New Year's Eve was also special to the Pharaohs," Yousef said. "They had the moon celebration."

"What did they do?" I asked.

"They honored it," Yousef said. "It was a special time. It still is."

"Lots of traditions handed down from the Pharaohs, I can see that," I said. "Thanks for making all the snacks and the soup. It'll be fun."

Yousef surprised me with the vegan tomato soup. He said he enjoyed the process of cutting the tomatoes, sautéing the onion, and blending it all together. Something about having a steaming hot cup of soup on the trail was so nourishing.

"I'm glad you dressed in layers, Yousef. You'll be surprised at how quickly you heat up."

We put on our backpacks and I handed him his poles. "Now just walk normally and use the poles for balance. You may have to widen your stance a bit."

"Easy," he said, walking around in a small circle. "I got it. Let's go."

We plodded through the darkness of Frontenac Park, our path ahead lit only by the moonlight and the occasional park light. It was beautiful even in this cold.

The large snowflakes fell gently and softly on my nose, then melted. Yousef brushed the snowflakes that collected on my hood. "I don't want you to turn into a snowman," he said.

"Snow woman," I said, brushing the snow off his hood.

Yousef smiled, his big, broad smile and white teeth showing faintly in the light.

There were hardly any prints in the snow, perhaps because they'd been covered up by the fresh snowfall and also because most Canadians had an aversion to snowshoeing in the cold on New Year's Eve.

"Yousef, when we were kids, we used to try to find shapes on the moon. My brother was so excited when he found a mouse," I said.

"We did that, too," Yousef said. "But we were looking for Pharaohs and Pyramids."

"You weren't!" I laughed.

"You'll never know," Yousef said, cutting ahead of me.

"Hey, wait, you're the newbie. You can't get ahead of me," I said, racing outside the track to pass him.

That lasted about two minutes.

"Oh, my god," I said, heaving. "I'm so tired. It's not fair that you're so much taller than I am with those long legs of yours. You take one step to two of mine."

"Little Janelle steps," he said, pointing to my tracks. Then, pointing to his tracks, he said, "Big Egyptian steps."

"This little Janelle needs to slow down a bit," I said.

"There's a cabin ahead," Yousef said. "I can almost see it clearly. We can have our cocoa and soup."

"That sounds good," I said, racing ahead of him.

Yousef cut ahead, then spread out his stance, blocking me from passing him. "Hey, you can't keep me back," I protested. "It's not fair."

"Life isn't fair, Janelle," he teased, stepping aside, then plodding in the snow beside me. "Come on, Janelle, I want to be near you."

I stood beside Yousef in the moonlight. "It's so beautiful, Janelle. I could never have imagined the silence at night, how stunning the moon is."

"It's spectacular, isn't it?"

"Let's enjoy it," he said. "Come slowly with me in the moonlight. The cabin is close by."

We snowshoed slowly into the night until we reached a small log cabin about the size of a large bedroom. Smoke puffs billowed out of the chimney. I loved the smell of a wood fire.

"Perfect timing, Yousef. My fingers are getting a little frozen."

"Popsicles that I shall eat," he said.

"You're crazy," I said.

"Just crazy for you," Yousef said. "Come on, let's go inside and warm up."

We leaned our snowshoes against the outside wall of the cabin. The cabin was sparsely furnished, with only a simple wooden table and bench on one side and a large stone fireplace and two chairs on the other. In one of the chairs was an older woman with gray hair wearing jeans and a heavy gray sweater. In the other chair was a gray-haired man, wearing a flannel lumberjack shirt, jeans, and winter boots, stoking the fire with an iron poker. Their coats and bags hung on the antler coat rack beside the door, and their snowshoes leaned against the wall. He briefly glanced at us and nodded. "Good evening," he said.

"Hello, how are you?" Yousef asked.

"Fine, thank you, stunning evening," he said. "Happy New Year!"

"Happy New Year," I greeted, smiling at them.

Yousef unloaded his backpack and eased mine off, placing them both on the table. He poured the soup into two cups and we toasted each other.

"Yousef, this is fantastic," I said. "I love it out here."

"It's your playground," he said. "Your oasis, right?"

"You got it. I love the peacefulness. With many of the animals gone or hibernating, it's you and the snow and the silent, tall trees overlooking."

After a few minutes, the cabin door creaked open and Mo walked in.

"Hi Janelle, how are you?" Mo asked, shaking the snow off his hat. He shook my hand. "Happy New Year!"

"What are you doing here?" I asked, shooting a sideways glance at Yousef. Yousef shrugged, shaking his head from side to side.

"Snowshoeing," Mo said.

"What a coincidence," I asked in disbelief. "On New Year's Eve?"

"Yes, in the neighborhood," Mo said.

Again I looked at Yousef, but he didn't acknowledge my questioning face. My wary eyes didn't even register with him.

"Is now the right time?" Mo asked.

Yousef nodded. "Now is the right time."

At that moment, the older man and woman stood up and approached us without saying a word. He was carrying a small notebook in his hand. "Are you ready?" he asked.

"We are, Jim," Yousef said.

Yousef smiled at the man and woman as well as Mo.

"Yousef, what's going on?" I asked.

Yousef knelt in front of me. He took a small red box out of his front coat pocket and opened it to show a shining diamond ring.

"Janelle," he said, "You've made me the happiest man ever. You've shown me adventures and parts of life I never would have done alone. You've made me a better man."

I tried to hold back the tears, but they busted out of my face.

"I promise to be a wonderful husband to you. Will you marry me?"

My voice quivered, "What did you do? You've been planning this the entire time."

Yousef smiled.

"What if I said I wanted to go to a pub tonight?" I cried. "And who are you?" I asked the older man and woman.

"Janelle, Jim is our officiant and his wife, a witness," Yousef said. "You told me you wanted to get married in the woods and I listened. Will you marry me?"

I wiped away my tears. Even though we'd been inside for an hour, my tongue was frozen along with the rest of me. How could Yousef be so sneaky? I never knew that he was capable of planning all this behind my back. He even convinced Mo to be a witness.

"What's the answer?" Mo asked.

"Janelle, don't make me nervous. Will you marry me?"

I ran into his arms. "Yes! Yes! Yes!"

"Thank you," he said.

Yousef slipped the ring on my left ring finger and hugged me.

"Now my eyes are so wet. They're going to freeze outside," I cried.

"Janelle, I'll wipe them dry. For the rest of your life." He reached over and wiped my tears away.

"There was no moon celebration in Egypt, was there?"

"That was a lie," Yousef said.

"You're not the only one who can teach about culture," Mo added.

"Yousef, you're incredible. I can't believe you planned everything this way. Mo, thank you for coming. Thank you for supporting us."

"It was my pleasure," Mo said. "I wanted to witness the beautiful event of my cousin, my best friend, getting married to the woman he loves."

"Shall we begin, then?" Jim asked.

We stood in front of him. Mo took out his cell phone and began to video.

Jim said, "We're gathered here today to celebrate the marriage of Yousef and Janelle. And to wish them from the bottom of our hearts, goodwill in their lifelong journey…"

I looked up at Yousef, and he looked into my eyes and soul. He held my hand in his.

Acknowledgements

With immense gratitude, we recognize the unwavering support of our friends and beta readers throughout the five-year journey of crafting this book.

Our heartfelt thanks go to Terry Fallis for his constant encouragement and continuous support, which helped us grow as writers and gave us the courage to continue. Our deepest appreciation goes to Jamal Saeed, a Syrian writer and refugee who has become one of Canada's precious gems, along with his wife, Rufaida Al Khabaz, for providing us with the outstanding support only close friends can offer.

We extend our thanks to the following mentors and friends who provided us with enduring support, encouragement, and thorough manuscript reviews: Alex Sawchyn, Steve Hunt, John S., Mustafa Marwan, David Lee, Greg Iannou, Brian Henry, Paul Stockton, Ursula Meier, Hashm N., Nancy Sewell, Raymond Michael Maday, Michelle Black, Irena Blodgett and Suzanne Lynn Reid.

Our gratitude also extends to the friends who read early excerpts and inspired us to persevere after the 130th iteration: Elaine and Mark, Dave and Marge Biggs, Elisabeth, Lory Kaufman, Steve C., Ellen Sands, the late Ray Argyle, Tamer Farag, Andrea R., Grace Murphy, Michael Bell, and Alice Rideout.

Author Bios

Pamela Paterson (pamthewriter.com) is a writer based in Kingston, Ontario. She has written seven books about ants, plants, kids, business, and computers, including two international best-sellers. This is her first novel.

Tarek Hussein (tarekthewriter.com) is a pharmacist and writer in Kingston, Ontario, with a lifelong passion for telling stories, writing songs, and taking pictures that capture the essence of life, from his native Cairo to several parts of the world that he has lived in or visited.

Post a Review

If you enjoyed this book, please consider telling others about it by posting a review in social media.

www.ingramcontent.com/pod-product-compliance
Lightning Source LLC
Chambersburg PA
CBHW030957210726
48290CB00007B/2356